"Champagne! How festive."

Polly's innocence made Flint smile. "One should always drink champagne at celebrations."

"Celebrations?"

"Aren't we celebrating the emergence of the new Polly Slater?"

"But I've never had champagne," Polly admitted, a little nervously.

"Well, now that you've launched on this life of glamour, I daresay you'll have quite a lot of it." Flint was teasing her.

"I won't object," Polly responded with exaggerated airiness.

Flint was suddenly serious. "Don't ever get blasé, Polly. Change the outside all you want, but don't change the inside. Please. Don't ever forget that glamorous women are a dime a dozen, but ladies like Polly Slater are a very rare breed."

Yes, she thought, a very rare breed, but not one pursued by men like Flint.

Celia Scott, originally from England, came to Canada for a vacation and began an "instant love affair" with the country. She started out in acting but liked romance fiction and was encouraged to make writing it her career when her husband gave her a typewriter as a wedding present. She now finds writing infinitely more creative than acting since she gets to act out all her characters' roles, and direct, too.

Books by Celia Scott

HARLEQUIN ROMANCE
2568—SEEDS OF APRIL
2638—STARFIRE
2735—WHERE THE GODS DWELL

Don't miss any of our special offers. Write to us at the following address for information on our newest releases.

Harlequin Reader Service
901 Fuhrmann Blvd., P.O. Box 1397, Buffalo, NY 14240
Canadian address: P.O. Box 603,
Fort Erie, Ont. L2A 5X3

A Talent for Loving

Celia Scott

Harlequin Books

TORONTO • NEW YORK • LONDON
AMSTERDAM • PARIS • SYDNEY • HAMBURG
STOCKHOLM • ATHENS • TOKYO • MILAN

Original hardcover edition published in 1986
by Mills & Boon Limited

ISBN 0-373-02831-8

Harlequin Romance first edition April 1987

CHAPTER ONE

'WHAT will you do now, then?' Marjorie Slater glared at her daughter, but Polly avoided her mother's eye and continued diligently stirring the cheese sauce she was making. 'Now that you're going to be unemployed again, what will you *do?*'

'I'll get another job, Mom,' Polly replied. 'It shouldn't be too difficult.'

'Another typing job?' Marjorie's voice was as sharp as a knife-edge.

'I guess so. Do you think this needs more milk?' She held the saucepan under her mother's nose.

'How should I know?' she snapped. 'Don't change the subject, Polly. Now that you've lost this job I want to know what you intend to do with your life.'

'I didn't exactly *lose* it, Mom, it was only a temporary one, for a couple of months, you knew that. Mr Ridley would have kept me on longer if he could.' She took her wide hazel gaze away from the saucepan to stare appealingly at her mother, but Marjorie was not about to be put off.

'Don't talk to me about that chauvinist,' she said, 'hiring girls just out of school so he can get away with paying minimum wages!'

Polly, who had liked Mr Ridley, and had felt sympathy for the mild little man who was struggling so bravely to keep his head above water, started to protest, but the older woman held up an imperious hand.

'I asked you a question, young woman,' she said. 'Do you mean to go on taking a series of temporary office jobs for the rest of your life? Or do you have other plans?' She pulled out a crumpled packet of cigarettes from the pocket of her denim jacket and lit one with a kitchen match. 'What do you want to do?' she said again, exasperated by her child's silence.

Before answering, Polly stooped to pick up the dead match her mother had thrown on the floor. 'I know what I'd *like* to do,' she said tentatively. 'I'd like to go to cooking school,' and when Marjorie snorted scornfully, she added, 'you did aske me what I *wanted* to do.'

'It's so *demeaning*. A typical female job.' Aggressively Marjorie blew smoke through her unpainted lips. 'A giant step backwards, Poll!'

Polly poured the velvety sauce over a dish of poached sole fillets and placed them under the grill. 'I don't think it's demeaning to cook,' she observed mildly, pushing back her tangled brown curls.

'You know very well what I mean,' her mother answered, and Polly's heart sank at the all too familiar hectoring note. 'All this fiddling about at the stove. It's *role playing,* that's what it is! A masculine ploy to keep women in a subservient position.'

'If I didn't fiddle about at the stove we'd starve to death,' Polly pointed out. 'You're not even capable of opening a can!'

Marjorie ignored this. 'I wouldn't mind so much,' she went on, 'if you had any real ambition. Wanted to open your own restaurant perhaps, or become a master chef. But no—I know you! If I let you train to become a cook you'll wind up slaving in some dreary kitchen working for an overbearing *man*. And enjoying it!' she added accusingly. 'You don't seem to have an ounce of normal drive. I don't know what's to become of you.' She stubbed out her barely smoked cigarette in a clean saucer and glared at her offspring.

'Poor old Mom!' Polly pitched the butt into the garbage and rinsed the saucer. 'I'm afraid you'll just have to face the fact that you're stuck with a washout. Apart from cooking there isn't a thing I want to do.' Deftly she drained the saucepan of new potatoes and dropped a knob of butter on them, gently shaking the pan. 'It's no good, Mom,' she said, 'you'll just have to reconcile yourself. I'm never going to be a high-powered business woman, I'm just not the type.'

Actually Polly sounded a good deal more cheerful than she felt. She loved her mother and would dearly have liked to please her, but she couldn't change her nature. She couldn't suddenly become a whizz at maths and take an engineering degree, or develop a sudden urge to become a nuclear physicist. What she longed for, in some deep recess in her heart, was to get married and look after a home filled with children and dogs and the general hurly-burly of a happy family. Do all the things, in fact, that Marjorie despised. And failing that, she wanted to learn to cook really well; maybe become a housekeeper. But she knew Marjorie wouldn't even *consider* such a life for her daughter. It's hard, Polly thought, being a failure at nineteen.

She removed the fish from the grill and set it, bubbling in its golden-brown sauce, on the kitchen table, then, taking a bowl of salad from the fridge, she started tossing it in the tarragon dressing she had prepared earlier. 'Would you divide up the potatoes, Mom?' she asked. 'Not too many for me.'

'Are you dieting again?' Marjorie scowled, stabbing at the potatoes with her fork.

'Well, I gained a bit over the weekend. It was the chocolate-peppermint cake that did me in.' Polly finished the salad and turned her attention to serving the fish. She wondered if she was in for yet another lecture about the immorality of trying to look like a sex-symbol when all that mattered in the world was the fight for female equality. The lecture didn't materialise, though, and the two women started their meal, each wrapped in her own thoughts.

Polly's were enough to give her indigestion, for, rightly or wrongly, she always felt that she had let her mother down. Wasn't it a fact that her very existence had made life difficult for Marjorie? To be a single parent, saddled with an illegitimate child at twenty, deserted by the man you had loved and hoped to marry, was no picnic. And if it hadn't been for Polly, no doubt they would never have emigrated from Great Britain ten years earlier. But Canada had been good to them. After travelling around the country for the first few years they had settled in Toronto, where Marjorie had landed a good job as legal secretary to a highly radical feminist lawyer. They had rented a pleasant little house in the Eglinton Avenue area of the city, and Polly had finished her schooling. Not brilliantly, it was true, but well enough after all that moving around. Although Marjorie would have liked some promise of brilliance. Some glimmer of driving ambition.

Polly took a quck look at her mother who was helping herself liberally to salad. 'I got a letter from Gran today,' she ventured, in an effort to establish a pleasanter dinner atmosphere. 'She sends you love and says she'll be writing to you later in the week.' Marjorie grunted. 'She sent me some birthday money too. So even if I don't get another job right away I'll still be able to contribute to the house.'

'If I know my mother she probably wants you to buy some kind of frippery.' She allowed herself a wintry smile, and Polly blushed, because her beloved gran had indeed stipulated "for something pretty!". 'We don't need your money, Poll. Deck yourself out like a man-trap, if that's what you want.' She pushed aside her empty plate and lit another cigarette.

'I think I'll wait until I've lost a bit of weight for that,' Polly replied. She collected the empty plates and started running the hot water. 'Do you want to wash or dry?' Her mother shrugged, so she handed her the drying-up towel, saying, 'You dry then, can't have you getting dishpan hands.' The smoke caught in Marjorie's throat, making her cough. 'You smoke too much, Mom,' Polly told her. 'You know that?'

Giving her daughter one of her rare smiles, Marjorie

stubbed out her cigarette. 'I'll quit next week,' she promised.

Polly peered through the kitchen window at the evening sunshine. 'I must say, July is turning into a super month,' she said. 'It's too nice to stay inside. Do you have any plans for this evening?'

Marjorie became brisk. 'I certainly do. I'm meeting some friends and we're going to spray-paint the new sexist ads for suntan lotion. The ones that have been put up in all the subway stations. Have you noticed them?'

Polly had. She had admired the model's svelte midriff, but she thought it prudent not to mention it. Instead she said, 'Don't get arrested, for goodness sake.' Her mother caused her frequent anxiety on this score.

'I don't suppose you'd like to join us?' Marjorie asked.

Polly shook her unruly brown curls. 'No, thanks, Mom, it's really not my scene. I plan to go for a long bike ride. It's good exercise. I might even lose a couple of pounds!'

In actual fact the bike ride wasn't quite as innocent as it sounded. Polly had a goal in view . . . a large grey stone mansion in Rosedale. There had been a lot of publicity when it had been rented by the famous Dexter Grant. The fabulously handsome actor had acquired the house as his Toronto base while he made a movie in the city. Polly had doted on him ever since she had seen him playing the lead in a romantic television series. Since he had moved into the house she had made daily excursions in the hope of catching a glimpse of her idol. Needless to say she said nothing of this to Marjorie, who would not have been very happy at the idea of Polly worshipping *any* male, whether it was from afar or not.

After her mother, clutching a spray-can of black paint, had left, Polly went upstairs to her bedroom to see if she could do anything about her appearance. She stared gloomily in the long mirror that was fastened to the back of her cupboard door. She had to admit that blue denim did nothing for her generous curves. But blue denim, or similar hardwearing fabrics, made up her entire wardrobe. Polly not only had a bad self-image, she also had a poor instinct about clothes. Convinced she was fat, when actually she was pleasingly plump, she didn't even try. And since Marjorie's assistance in choosing flattering garments was nil, Polly's meagre wardrobe consisted of jeans and sturdy skirts, topped by tee-shirts that squeezed her full breasts, or boyish blouses that hung shapelessly.

Sighing, she removed her stiff navy wrap-skirt and tan cotton top and stood in bra and panties looking at her reflection. She longed to be five foot ten and thin as a rail, but she was five foot nothing, with firm, full breasts and wide, rounded hips. Her legs were shapely, but short, her tummy ever so slightly curved. Blind to her flawless white skin, so velvety it looked like fresh cream, she frowned at her image in the mirror. Two weeks ago she had tried to improve her appearance by cutting bangs with her nail scissors. It hadn't worked. Now the mass of curly brown hair fell over her forehead, obscuring her fine tawny eyes, so that she peered out at the world like a cautious little animal peering from its lair.

She reached into the cupboard and pulled out the first thing that came to hand . . . a stiff cotton shirt-dress checked in orange and brown. Slamming the cupboard door, she groped under the bed for her battered black sandals. They were on top of the shoebox containing her contraband paperback romance novels. Contraband because she knew the fuss Marjorie would make if she suspected that her daughter enjoyed such "sentimental rubbish". Guiltily, for she was not a deceitful girl by nature, she rearranged the pink nylon bedspread so that the box was hidden.

She thought she would tie her hair back, it was cooler that way, but the only ribbon she could lay her hands on was of scarlet velvet. With a defiant gesture she tied back her thick hair with it anyway. This exposed more of her face which to her despair was round, with a scattering of freckles over her tip-tilted nose, like a wash of gold. 'And Mom accuses me of trying to look like a sex-symbol,' she muttered to herself, 'Fat chance!'

The journey to Rosedale took Polly about three-quarters of an hour. She had worked out a route so that she could cycle part of the way through one of the many ravines that cut through the city, a wooded tunnel where bird song vied with the hum of downtown traffic. This evening the slanting rays of sun gilded the tall trees that were coming into their full summer glory. Sometimes joggers ran doggedly along the path. Many had personal stereo earphones clamped over their heads, their faces blank, eyes glazed as the tinned music dinned into their skulls.

Pedalling along as fast as she could, Polly thanked her lucky stars again that Marjorie had decided to put down roots in this lovely city with its acres of green parkland and miles of sparkling lakefront. If they couldn't live in the country, which was Polly's secret dream, Toronto was the next best thing. If she shut out the constant hum of traffic she could have been cycling down a country lane.

She reached the turn-off and started to climb the steep hill that led to her destination. The Rosedale mansion stood back off the road in its own grounds. It was surrounded by a wrought iron fence. There was a curved sweep of drive, and to the right of the house was a privet-enclosed swimming pool. The hedge was nearly six feet high, but Polly had discovered that if she stood up on the pedals of her bike she could just see over it. It meant she had to cycle on the grass verge, not on the road, but there were very few people around at this hour, so this unorthodox behaviour usually went unnoticed.

She wheeled her bike on to the grass and started cycling up and down beside the fence, standing up on the pedals trying to see into the grounds. She heard a splash, and then the sound of someone swimming. It was the first time there had ever been a sign of life at the mansion, and her heartbeat quickened with excitement.

Wobbling perilously on the uneven grass she tiptoed higher. Her attention was focused on the pool area, so she didn't notice that she was coming to the edge of the grass, where it met the drive. Nor did she notice an orange BMW coming out of the gates.

Her front wheel rolled on to the gravel and the BMW hit it. Polly was whirled into the air. She landed on her side on the drive, her skirt pulled up on her thighs, and a great deal of rough gravel embedded in her bare flesh. Her bike was still trapped by its front wheel under the orange car which had come to a halt. A young man, his white face crowned by a thatch of red hair, slammed out of the driver's seat.

'Are you all right?' He looked as shaken as she felt. 'Are you badly hurt?'

'I . . . I don't think so.' Experimentally she moved her leg. 'Nothing seems to be broken. I'm just grazed.' In an attempt at modesty she tried pulling her skirt down over her thigh and winced when the cotton brushed her torn skin.

'Where the hell did you come from?' the young man demanded. 'You came at me out of nowhere!'

'I was riding on the grass . . . beside the fence,' she explained sheepishly.

The young man glared at her. He was leaning over her now, and she could almost count the hairs of his short red beard. Polly had always disliked beards.

'You're not supposed to ride on the bloody grass!' he snarled. His eyes, which were a startling shade of blue, looked red-rimmed and strained. She wondered if he had been drinking and her heart sank at the thought of dealing with a drunk on top of everything else. She tried a surreptitious sniff to see if she could detect alcohol on his breath. 'You're not going to cry, are you?' he asked unsympathetically.

'Certainly not.' She pulled herself up into a sitting position, for she felt like a fool lying on the drive being harangued by this unpleasant man. But the effort made her grazed flesh sting, and tears of pain flooded her eyes.

'Crying won't help you,' her tormentor informed her. 'Perhaps now you'll leave the sidewalks to the pedestrians.'

'I wasn't on the sidewalk. I was on the *grass*!' She was getting fed up with this man. Did he expect her to lie at his feet, abject and bleeding, for the rest of the evening?

He ignored her. 'You shouldn't have a bike if you're frightened to use the roadway,' he said.

'I'm not frightened to use the roadway,' Polly snapped back. 'I usually do. I was only riding on the verge in front of this house because I wanted to . . . well, I wanted to . . . to see in.' She was aware that this didn't sound too good.

'See in? Why? Are you planning a burglary?'

'Of course not. I wanted to see . . . hoped I might catch a glimpse of . . . of Dexter Grant. I'm a great admirer of his,' she finished lamely.

'Oh, lord in heaven defend us! A groupie!' He looked at her with infinite distaste. 'Why couldn't you have just waited at the studio to see him, like everyone else?'

'I never thought of it,' she confessed.

'Well, next time you want to gawk at your hero I suggest you try using your brains for a change. That way you'll avoid hurling yourself under the wheels of my car.'

'I didn't hurl myself. You ran me *down*!' Her voice rose a decibel. 'You might at least say you're sorry.'

'Why should I? It was entirely your own fault. Mooning over fences when you should have been looking where you were going!' He pulled at the sleeve of his disreputable khaki shirt. Now that she had had time to collect herself she realised that he had an altogether rumpled appearance. He had squatted down beside her, in order to shout at her more effectively, she supposed, and she could see that the knees of his jeans were almost worn through. He wore ancient suede boots that looked as if the upper and the sole were about to part company, and his thick hair stood on end in an angry crest. She doubted it had seen a comb for days.

What she couldn't figure out was what on earth this kind of tramp was doing on the grounds of Dexter Grant's rented house? Maybe he had made some sort of delivery. But in that case what was he doing using the main driveway? Surely a mansion as luxurious as this had a tradesmen's entrance?

'I wasn't mooning,' she said. 'I was just . . . observing. And if it comes to that . . .' she blinked up at him triumphantly from beneath her heavy fringe, 'if it comes to that, what were *you* doing using the front driveway? How do you explain that?'

He stared at her, mystified. 'Have you lost your marbles?' he said. 'Did you hit your head when you fell? Why in heck shouldn't I use the drive?'

Before she could tell him to get down off his high horse and stop being so righteously indignant, they were interrupted.

'What the hell's going on, Flint?' said an unmistakable male voice.

Polly's heart did a flip-flop. She had heard that voice a hundred times before, drawling lazily in countless love scenes, making his fans' hearts melt, just as Polly's was melting now. Dexter Grant! There he was, standing at the entrance to the pool. He was wearing a pair of rather startling silver swimming trunks, a towel slung across his tanned shoulders. He was dripping wet and his blond hair was turned to a pewter colour by the water. 'What's going on, Flint?' he repeated, and started to walk carefully over the grass towards them.

Polly gazed up at him, too mesmerised to utter a word. The magic moment was broken by the redhaired man.

'It's okay, Dex. This . . .' he cast a scathing look at the recumbent girl, 'this *chick* cycled herself into my car. It's not serious.'

Polly's theory about deliverymen and driveways crumbled like dust, for no deliveryman would use Dexter Grant's first name with such casual ease.

'You poor kid!' said the actor, directing the full power

of his grey eyes at Polly, who was glad she was not on her feet as she was sure she would have fainted with pleasure. 'Are you badly hurt? Should we call an ambulance?'

'Don't panic,' the man called Flint said, 'there's no need for dramatics. Give me a hand to get her into the house. Her cuts need cleaning, that's all.'

'My knees hurt,' said Polly, glaring. It was all very well for him to dismiss her grazed legs so arbitrarily. He wasn't the one who had been run down.

'Hang in there, kiddo!' At least Dexter Grant looked suitably sympathetic. 'Do you think you can walk?'

'Of course she can walk,' Flint said crisply, 'once we get her on her feet.' He hooked his hands under her armpits and stood upright, dragging her up with him. He had very strong arms, she noticed, and despite his leanness his shoulders were broad and muscular.

'Now you get on the other side of her, Dex, and help me take her to the downstairs washroom.' He was clearly familiar with the layout of the house.

Dutifully Dexter looped his naked arm round her waist and the three of them made their way to the back of the house. Polly was delightfully aware of the famous actor's body close to her. But he was shorter than she had imagined. The odious Flint was at least four inches taller. *He* held her arm in a vice-like grip that made her feel like a criminal being marched off to the cells. She had a brief glimpse of a gleaming stainless steel and teak kitchen before being lugged into a small washroom, where Flint unceremoniously pushed her down on to the lid of the toilet.

'Let's have a look at those grazes,' he ordered, nodding at her skirt, which, she noticed, was dirty and had a rip in it.

Feeling extremely self-conscious, she raised the grubby material. Both knees were bleeding, and various scratches marred the silky texture of her thighs. The side of one hand was bleeding too, and she had a nasty bruise on her elbow.

'You poor sweetie!' said Dexter Grant. 'You sure did hit the dust. How did it happen?'

'She wasn't looking where she was going . . . trying to get a glimpse of you. She's a fan,' Flint informed him wryly.

Polly's normally pink cheeks turned scarlet. She was hideously embarrassed and she cursed this dreadful Flint from the depths of her heart. But Dexter Grant was obviously delighted.

'Aw, sweetie! That's cute. I like that,' he grinned.

Flint cut in. 'Trust you! Now, let's cut out the admiration society and get to work cleaning her up!' He made it sound as if they were about to start work on a dirty boat. 'You fetch a basin and some disinfectant while I park my car. It's still blocking the drive.'

'Will you be okay for a while, sweetie?' Dexter asked her. 'You won't faint if you're left alone?'

She shook her head, realising that her ribbon must have come off when she fell, for her riotous mane of nutmeg-coloured hair swung over her face.

'If you do feel faint just put your head between your knees,' said the charmless Flint. 'We shan't be long.' He marched off.

'Don't go away, sweetie,' Dexter Grant said, with what Polly hoped was uncharacteristic winsomeness.

'I'll be fine,' she assured his departing bare back. 'I love sitting in strange washrooms!'

She took stock of her surroundings. There were all the usual fittings, very modern and luxurious. The wash basin was gold-coloured, with an elaborate-looking set of taps. The walls were papered in avocado green, with a glittery free-form design in gold; there was a thick pile avocado carpet on the floor, and lots of fluffy green and gold towels; even the guest soaps in a shallow gold steel dish were in the same shades. This made the single cyclamen, planted in a green pottery container, blaze like a pink flame on the window ledge. The room was like an illustration in *Architectural Digest*. Trendy, glossy, and a little bit inhuman.

'Action stations, sweetie!' Dexter Grant, dressed now in a black judo robe with gold satin cuffs and sash, deposited a basin, some cotton-wool and a bottle of iodine on the carpeted floor. 'These emergencies always happen on the staff's night out, don't they?' he observed.

His hair was now dry and swept off his face in ash-blond waves. He was so handsome Polly couldn't take her eyes off him. She was star-struck, tongue-tied, and she looked a total wreck.

Flint burst into the small room. He held out her crumpled red-velvet ribbon as if it were the tail of a particularly repellent dead animal. 'This yours?' he asked. Wordlessly she took it from him and stuffed it in her pocket.

She couldn't help noticing that he had shapely hands, with artistic fingers and well-kept nails, which didn't fit in with his generally scruffy look.

'I hope you live near here,' he said.

'I . . . I don't,' she faltered 'Why?'

'Because you won't be able to cycle anywhere. Your front wheel's buckled. It's the subway for you for the next few days.'

'Oh no!' wailed Polly.

Dexter smiled at her reassuringly. 'Flint here can drive you home. Where do you live?'

'Near Eglinton and Yonge,' she told them, then gasped when Flint started to swab her right knee with some wet absorbent cotton.

'Hold still,' Flint said, 'I don't want to drip on your skirt.' In spite of his general surliness he was unexpectedly gentle. He reached for another piece of cotton wool. 'Why don't *you* drive her?' he said to the actor, who was leaning negligently against the door.

'No way, man! Too many lines to learn,' Dexter answered.

'Too lazy to get dressed you mean,' remarked Flint, giving the black-robed figure a lop-sided grin. He had nice firm lips hidden in that red beard. And nice teeth, uneven, but startlingly white.

'Lazy!' Dexter spread his hands wide, 'give me a break! I'm making a movie, remember? I'm *exhausted*, man!'

'Of course I'm not tired at all,' Flint said bitterly. He looked at Polly and she saw that he did indeed have dark circles, like sooty thumb-prints, beneath his eyes. 'Eglinton's just too far out of my way,' he said, 'I'm afraid I can't drive you home.'

'We'll put you in a taxi, sweetie,' the actor informed her. 'You won't mind that, will you?'

'Not at all.' She straightened her shoulders. She hoped she sounded dignified, although it was difficult to be dignified sitting on a toilet-seat lid.

'Now, this is going to sting,' said Flint, wielding the iodine bottle 'Try not to yelp.'

'I'm not in the habit of yelping,' she said, offended. But when the brown liquid stained her broken skin she had to use every ounce of will power not to cry out.

'You know something?' Dexter declared, 'I hate the sight of blood. I think I'll go to the study and pour us all a drink. Join me there when you're finished.'

'No drink for me,' said Flint, dabbing away at her hand now with the cotton-wool. 'If I drink alcohol I'll drop in my tracks.'

Drop in his tracks, will he? Polly thought, maybe he does have a drinking problem after all. Maybe he's been on a bender and that's why he looks such a mess.

'What about you, sweetie?' Dexter asked her. 'What will you have?'

'Some sort of soft drink if she's got any sense,' Flint volunteered. 'Anyway, I doubt she's old enough to drink.'

'I certainly am old enough!' Polly was livid. Who did this man think he was? Treating her as if she was scarcely out of the cradle! 'I'll have a Scotch and soda please,' she said grandly.

'Scotch and soda it is!' said Dexter as he departed.

Polly had never drunk whisky in her life, the occasional glass of wine was the extent of her alcoholic experience. But Scotch and soda sounded sophisticated, and she was damned if she was going to let this Flint character dictate to her.

She fixed him with a haughty stare. '*I* don't have a drinking problem,' she said.

He looked puzzled. 'I should hope not. Now, a dab of iodine on the hand and we're finished.'

She held out her hand stoically, but the iodine stung so much that in spite of her discipline her amber-coloured eyes filled with tears.

He glanced at her face briefly and said gruffly, 'All over now. You should be as right as rain in a couple of days.'

Courtesy made her say 'Thank you', but she was still burning with resentment at his high-handed attitude.

'The study's the second door on the left when you go down the hall,' said Flint, gathering up the bowl, cotton wool and iodine. 'I'll leave you to find your own way. Then we must ring for your cab.' He looked at her sternly before loping out of the washroom.

Stiffly Polly stood up and dared a quick glance in the mirror. She looked worse than she had feared. Her hair was an untidy bird's nest, her face was drawn, and the freckles stood out on her skin. And her dress, which was not flattering at the best of times, was creased and made her look fat. Miserably, she pulled her fingers through her bangs in a futile attempt to smooth them, then, pinching her cheeks hard to give them some colour, she took a deep breath and left on her search for the study.

She found it without difficulty, and after a tentative knock, poked her head round the door. Dexter was sprawled in an armchair of soft grey leather, looking at a video machine. She looked at it too and was entranced to see his handsome face flickering on the screen; he was playing a highly emotional scene with an equally famous actress. Polly remembered the scene well, she had watched the original programme, and all the re-runs, and she probably knew the lines by now as well as the actors did.

Dexter leaned across to a silver tray that stood on a chrome and glass table. 'Your drink, sweetie-pie,' he said, indicating a heavy glass, containing a generous portion of Scotch whisky. He put two ice cubes in it and started to pour from a bottle of soda water. 'Say when!'

'When!' said Polly immediately, not having the faintest idea of the right proportions.

He handed her the glass and raised his vodka and tonic in a toast, before returning his attention to the screen.

She took a sip of the whiskey and nearly gagged. She had never tasted anything so awful in her life! Furtively she looked around to see if there was a vase or a plant, where she could stealthily empty away this filthy stuff, but there was nothing of the sort in this elegant, uncluttered room. Dexter turned again in her direction and she forced herself to take a huge swallow. She curled her toes *hard*, smiled gamely, and managed to keep it down. After the burning sensation had worn off she did feel a pleasant glow steal over her, and she relaxed a little against the scarlet upholstery of the love-seat Dexter had waved her into.

'I hope you don't mind this, honey?' He indicated the flickering screen. 'It's the way I learn my craft. I watch videos of myself in different roles.'

'You must have a Ph.D. by now, then!' Flint was at the open door. He pressed a switch and a bank of track lights came on; Polly noticed that it was now dark outside. He leaned against the door-jamb, a mug of black coffee in his hand, and gave another of his lopsided grins. 'Admit it, Dex! You love looking at that handsome mug of yours. The learning is of secondary interest.'

Breathlessly Polly waited for the great Dexter Grant to cut this impertinent creature down to size, but the actor merely grinned back and said, 'Okay, okay! I admit it. I love my neat profile.'

Polly leaned towards him, emboldened by another gulp of Scotch. 'It's not just your profile, Mr. Grant,' she said earnestly, 'it's your talent too. I've seen everything you've ever done, and I think you're the greatest actor in the world.' She leaned further and repeated firmly, 'In the entire *world* !'

'Behold a lady of intelligence!' Dexter looked very pleased. 'Er . . . what did you say your name was?'

'We didn't get around to introductions,' Polly explained, 'I knew who you were right away of course . . . but I'm Paula Slater . . . only everyone calls me Polly . . .'

'Pretty Polly!' said Dexter. Insincerely, Polly couldn't help thinking. 'Pretty Polly, meet my old pal, Flint McGregor.' He waved at the tall figure in the doorway. 'For Pete's sake sit down, Flint. You look like a cop about to make an arrest. Stop *looming*!' Formalities over, he resumed, 'Now, Polly, which of my movies have you enjoyed most?'

Before she had a chance to launch into a minute account of everything he had ever done, she was interrupted by Flint.

'Before this admiration session gets under way, I phoned for a cab. It should be here in fifteen minutes.' He flung himself into a grey leather chair opposite Polly and glowered at her.

Not bothering to answer this, Polly turned to Dexter and proceeded to tell him how marvellous she thought his last television series had been.

Flint stretched out his long legs and concentrated on staying awake. The five hour delay in Tehran on his flight home from India had really added to his jet-lag. The way he figured it, he had now been without sleep for something like thirty hours! If it hadn't been for this wretched star-struck idiot he would have been home in bed by now. But he couldn't leave before he'd seen her safely off the premises. And if she kept on like this, dishing out the flattery, Dex was liable to send the taxi away just to hear more of the same. He was so naive sometimes.

For all they knew she might deliberately have engineered the accident, just to gain access. She might be planning to sue! But he knew Dex! He was fool enough to keep her here, alone with him, for no other reason than to drink in the adulation. He never seemed to get enough. Never thinking that she might suddenly turn nasty, scream rape or something; cause all kinds of scandal; or try blackmail. And while Dex might be a conceited ass at times, he didn't deserve that. So once more his old pal Flint McGregor would have to look out for him.

It was lousy timing though. After a gruelling six weeks on an assignment photographing in Nepal, all he had wanted to do was to come in from the airport, pick up his car from Dex's garage, then drive home to his farm in Caledon. He couldn't wait to climb out of his travel-stained clothes and into his bed. He *had* to get some sleep! He had a wicked schedule ahead of him. He had to develop all his Nepal pictures *and* write the article to go with them, and he had a deadline to meet for the magazine. Blast that girl! He would never get caught up at this rate.

He shifted his aching bones in the soft leather chair and squinted over at Polly, who was now rapturously listening while Dexter gave her a blow-by-blow account of the difficulties he was having with his current film.

Flint found it hard to place this girl! She acted like an entire Dexter Grant fan-club, but he had been around Dexter since their high-school days, long enough to recognise the type of girl who became a fanatical fan, a hanger-on, and this Polly what's-her-name didn't fit the mould. First of all, she didn't look right. She was downright dowdy. No groupie with an ounce of self-respect would be caught dead in a dress like hers. And while her face was quite pretty, what you could see of it under all that hair, she hadn't even bothered to wear lip-gloss. And this idiot didn't even have a purse, let alone an autograph book. Something just didn't jell!

To his immense relief the doorbell chimed just then, breaking into Dexter's stream of reminiscences.

'That'll be the taxi' Flint unwound his tall figure from the confines of the chair and waited for Polly to stand up too. 'Time to break up the party.'

'It's been wonderful meeting you, Mr. Grant,' Polly said 'I'll never forget it.'

'"Dexter", sweetie-pie. Don't be so formal' His handsome face smiled up at her.

'She's going to need some money for the cab,' Flint reminded him, 'do you have any?'

'Not in my robe, man!' Dexter laughed.

Sighing, Flint reached into the pocket of his jeans and extracted a twenty-dollar bill. 'Here!' He thrust it at Polly.

She shook her head. 'That's too much.' The last thing she wanted was to be in Flint's debt.

'It's the only Canadian money I have' He pushed the bill into her hand. 'Don't be difficult!'

'What about my bike?' she asked, suddenly remembering her shattered bicycle.

'I've left a note for Dexter's house-boy, Wai, he'll phone the cycle repair shop tomorow. They'll pick it up and fix it for you. It'll be in Dexter's name,' said Flint.

'Good old Flint! He thinks of everything,' Dexter smiled. 'It's been lovely talking to you Polly. It's people like you who make my work worthwhile.' He rose to his feet to accompany her to the front door. 'Why don't you drop by next Sunday? For tea, maybe,' he suggested, 'and I could show you some more of my videos. We'll get the repair people to deliver your bike back here. You can pick it up then.'

'Wouldn't it be easier for her to get it from the shop?' Flint said, with a warning look, which Dexter ignored.

'Don't be dumb, Flint! She'd like to see some more of my films. Wouldn't you?' He turned to Polly who nodded enthusiastically. 'She can give me your twenty dollars then, too. Then we'll all be happy. He beamed at her, and, speechless with joy, she beamed back.

By now they had reached the heavy front door. Flint opened it and firmly pushed Polly out on to the front steps. He turned back to his friend in the hall and she heard him hiss, 'For God's sake be careful, Dex. You don't know anything about this kid. You don't want to be saddled with some mindless flake who could become a nuisance.'

'But she's a honey!' Dexter protested 'Besides, I need a bit of extra admiration these days. The grind of this damn movie is really getting to me.'

'Well, don't say I didn't warn you. She strikes me as the type that's hard to get rid of.'

Polly felt the rosy colour flood her face, staining even the tips of her ears. If she had a gun she would have had no hesitation in shooting this hateful man dead on the spot!

However, Dexter Grant paid no attention to his friend. He came out on to the steps and put his arm round her shoulder. Walking with her to the waiting cab he made a handsome, but incongruous figure in his short black judo robe.

'Sunday then, sweetie!' he said, 'about threeish. Okay?'

'Fine . . . wonderful . . .' she stuttered. She wondered how she would have reacted if someone had told her earlier that before the night was out Dexter Grant would have his arm around her shoulder. She would have laughed, probably, for it was beyond her wildest imaginings that she would even *meet* her favourite movie star . . . and now he had invited her to tea!

She climbed into the back seat of the taxi and gave her address to the cabbie. Rolling down the window, she said, 'Thank you for the drink . . . and everything. It was almost worth being run down, just for the pleasure of meeting you.' She pointedly ignored Flint, who was standing on the top step, with his hands jammed into his pockets, his face like a thunder cloud.

'You're a honey, Pretty Polly! Take care now. *Ciao*!' The actor waved and went up the front steps to where Flint was waiting.

As the cab drove off Polly twisted in her seat to catch a last glimpse of her favourite star, but she was out of luck. All she saw were Flint's broad shoulders and gesticulating arms as he said something—almost certainly unpleasant—to Dexter's retreating back. She gave a sigh of exasperation, then brightened. Never mind! She had Sunday with her idol to look forward to. It was unlikely she would run across Flint McGregor again, and as far as she was concerned that was just fine! She would forget him. Put him out of her mind.

But to her anoyance that was easier said than done, for every time she conjured up an image of Dexter, Flint was there too. Like a testy ghost who refused to be exorcised.

CHAPTER TWO

THE time until Sunday passed on two levels for Polly. One fast, and one excruciatingly slow. She seemed to be collecting her last pay-packet and becoming unemployed again in no time flat, but the days until the moment when she would see Dexter dragged. But at least, she comforted herself, it gave her injured knees a chance to heal.

When Polly had arrived home the night of her accident Marjorie had not yet returned, so she had been able to get to bed without having to face her mother. In the morning, disguising her stiff legs as best she could, she made light of the incident, telling Marjorie that she had met with a minor accident on her bike, and that "some people in a nearby house" had assisted her. She didn't go into any more details, and Marjorie didn't press her.

Marjorie was still annoyed with her daughter, and was punishing her by putting her in a conversational deep freeze. If she had only known this suited Polly very well, since it left it her time to daydream about Dexter and Sunday's meeting!

The heat had been building all week and by Sunday it was both hot and humid, with a sky the colour of dirty linen. After her usual gloomy examination of her wardrobe she settled on her denim wrap-skirt and a brown cotton blouse, because it was the coolest thing she had. She had toyed with the idea of buying a new dress for the occasion, but had felt it would have been too extravagant in view of her unemployed status. She had washed her hair that morning, but the damp air had made it so curly she could scarcely tug her comb through it. In an attempt at tidiness, and in a effort to stay cool, she plaited it into a thick braid that hung down her back in a gleaming rope. Then she polished her sturdy black leather sandals, slung her nylon bag over her shoulder, and set off, feeling quite numb with expectation.

At the entrance to Dexter's house she stopped in her tracks. The drive was clogged with parked cars, people spilled out of the house and sprawled on the lawn, and the swimming-pool echoed with splashes and laughter.

Had she mistaken the day? No way! "Sunday . . . threeish" was engraved on her heart in letters of gold! Her first instinct was to turn and run, but practicability stopped her. She needed her bicycle. She couldn't afford to go on taking public transport. Steeling herself, she made her way to the open front door. A girl dressed in white satin shorts, a wisp of turquoise cotton over her small breasts, was coming from the area of the kitchen. Her brown midriff—the colour of ancient Etruscan terracotta—looked very familiar.

'Can I help you?' the girl asked, her dark eyes sweeping over Polly, taking in the stiff blue skirt and mannish shirt.

'Is Mr. Grant anywhere around? I've come about my

bike ... ' Gone were all thoughts of invitations of tea.

'Your *bike* ?' The girl raised her beautifully pencilled eyebrows.

'Yes, it's been repaired ... I had an accident.' Suddenly Polly knew why this lovely girl's middle was familiar. This was the girl in the suntan advertisement! The advertisement that was on every subway station in Toronto. The advertisement that had driven Majorie into a frenzy of spray-painting!

'Dex!' the girl shouted back into the region of the kitchen. 'Dex! There's someone here to see you about a bicycle.' She looked back at Polly. Her gaze wasn't unfriendly, but she didn't invite her to cross the threshold.

Dexter Grant, two tall frosted tumblers in his hands, backed out of the kitchen swing-doors. He passed one of the tumblers to the dark girl. 'Here you are, Sable—your rum and O.J. Now, what's this about a bike?'

The girl indicated Polly standing hot and embarrassed on the doorstep. 'She says she's come to pick up her bike.' She giggled, 'What *have* you been up to, Dexter?'

The movie star took a step towards Polly, and to her dismay she could tell from the blank look in his eyes that he didn't remember her from a hole in the ground! Cheeks burning, she said, 'Remember, Mr. Grant? I was run down outside your house. You sent me home in a taxi, and——'

'Sure! I remember now!' The penny had dropped. 'You hurt your knees. Er... ' he scrambled desperately for her name, 'Dolly, isn't it?'

'Polly—Polly Slater. I'm sorry to disturb you, but——'

'Hell, you're not disturbing me, sweetie! Grab yourself a drink and join the party.'

'No, really—I'll just get my bike.' Under the disappointment she was beginning to feel a slow burn of indignation.

'I wouldn't know where it is, honey.' She should have known that he was above such mundane things. 'Wai might know, but he's cooking right now. Go and get a drink like a good girl, and when he's finished you can ask *him*. Sable will show you where the bar is.' He flashed his famous smile at the willowy brunette and returned to the kitchen, leaving the two women alone in the hall.

'Honestly! He really is the living *end*!' the girl exclaimed. She came closer, and with a pang Polly saw that she was about five foot ten, slender as a thread, and much, much more beautiful than she appeared on the billboards. 'My name's Sable Winter,' she said, smiling, 'and you're Polly—right?' Polly nodded. 'You must excuse his lousy manners,' she jerked her head back towards the interior of the house. Her jet black hair was cut short in a sleek cap. 'I don't think he's ever been properly house-trained. *And* of course he's an actor! Need I say more?' she smiled. It was an infectious grin, and in spite of her disappointment Polly grinned back. She liked this lovely girl, who was very friendly, now that the first cautious introductions had been made.

'Let's go and get that drink,' suggested Sable. She led the way across the lawn, her long brown legs scissoring to and fro.

'No—really. I don't think . . . ' Polly bleated as she tried to keep up. Chasing after this glorious creature, she felt like a tug wallowing behind a sleek liner.

Sable disregarded her protests, and soon they passed through the gate to the pool area, where the bar was set up. 'Here we are,' said Sable, 'name your poison.'

The man behind the bar was stooping to open a crate of soft drinks, so that all Polly could see at first was a pair of wide shoulders and a glint of red hair. Then he straightened up. A pair of electric blue eyes looked straight into Polly's.

'Well, well, well!' Flint said, 'if it isn't demon biker!'

'Oh, you've met, have you?' said Sable. 'Then I'll leave her in your care, Flint, and go help Dex in the kitchen.' For all her friendliness she seemed very anxious to get away. 'Bye, now!' she trilled, waving an exquisitely manicured hand.

'As I recall, you drink Scotch and soda, is that right?' There was a glint of malice in Flint's blue eyes.

Polly shrieked, 'No!' then recovered herself and added, with what she hoped was dignity, 'it's—er—it's a little too early for me yet. Maybe a ginger ale, or some soda water?'

Flint poured the bubbly ginger ale into a long slim glass, dropped ice into it and handed it to her. She had to admit that if it hadn't been for his distinctive colouring she would hardly have recognised him. The beard was gone, and his wild mane, though not exactly sleek, had been cut and tamed into submission. He was dressed in a faded blue shirt and a pair of cream linen pants. Not exactly trendy, but pressed and crisp as newly minted money.

'I can't offer you tea as promised,' he said, 'so this will have to do.'

She was surprised that he had remembered. It was more than Dexter had done. 'I really only want to collect my bike. But nobody knows where it is. Oh, and to pay you back!' She fumbled in her purse and pulled out an envelope containing a twenty-dollar bill.

'Thanks!' He stuffed the envelope into his shirt pocket. 'You got home all right, then?'

Before she could reply, a bikini-clad girl came up to the bar. She held out her empty glass, and laughing up at Flint said, 'More of the same, please, Flint baby.' She did not acknowledge Polly's presence by so much as the flicker of an eyelash. 'When are you going to bare that gorgeous torso and join me in the pool?'

'Not this time around.' He was pleasant, but not encouraging. 'I didn't expect a party, so I didn't bring swimming trunks.'

'Swim without them, lover,' leered the girl. '*I* won't object.'

Flint started to pour from a bottle of white wine.

'Excuse me,' he said to Polly, 'I got stuck with this job when Wai went in to prepare the food, and it doesn't leave much time for socialising.'

'I don't expect you to socialise,' Polly replied, walking away from the bar.

Flint called after her, 'See you later!'

'I doubt it!' She gave him a stiff little smile. 'As soon as I find my bike I'm off.'

She marched resolutely through the chattering crowd. She was very upset. For some reason the discourteous behaviour of the scantily clad girl seemed to be the last straw, and Polly had to swallow hard to control her anger. She found a garden chair under a tree that grew close to the wall of the house, a good distance from the party, and she sat there watching the antics of the careless, beautiful people, who reminded her of a flock of brightly coloured birds as they laughed and played together.

She was utterly miserable. her ginger ale tasted sickly, and the oppressive weather was beginning to make her head ache. She shifted uncomfortably in the chair. Her whole body felt sticky with the heat. And to think she had been dreaming all week of Sunday afternoon! She had imagined herself sitting again in the study, a tea-tray on the chrome and glass table between them, as Dexter told her of his experiences in the theatre. It would have been the beginning of a friendship between herself and the actor. With him as mentor and her in the role of adoring acolyte. Well, there wasn't much chance of that, he hadn't even remembered her name, let alone his invitation!

Suddenly she made up her mind to collect her bicycle another day. She would leave—now! She wouldn't stay here another moment.

She poured the ginger ale on to the ground, and, carefully leaving the empty glass on a nearby window-sill, she almost ran to the front gate, where she collided headlong with Flint McGregor.

'Don't you *ever* look where you're going?' he said, steadying her.

'Sorry—I was just leaving   I didn't see you.'

'Did you find your bike?'

'No . . . no. I'll come back another day and get it.' She tried to free herself, but he kept his hands on her shoulders and looked intently into her face.

'Let's go look for it,' he said, turning her back to the house. She protested, but he merely tucked her arm firmly under his. 'Come on! Don't dawdle.'

They entered the hall, which was carpeted with pale grey broadloom. A marble pedestal holding a large black onyx egg stood in a recess, but apart from this the place was stark and bare of ornaments.

Flint pushed her through the swing doors into the kitchen. This room was as brightly lit as a lamp show-room. A track of spotlights was trained on the working area, and the illuminated chrome and steel made Polly blink with the reflected glare. An Oriental man, wrinkled as a walnut, was taking a tray of hot hors d'oeuvres from a wall oven. Dexter and Sable were sitting at the large glass kitchen table, which was loaded with an assortment of bottles and mixes—replenishments for the poolside bar, presumably. They looked up as Flint, pushing the reluctant Polly ahead of him, entered.

'Hi! Need more booze at the bar?' Dexter asked his friend.

'I wouldn't know. I let some other sucker take over that job,' said Flint, 'I just dropped by for some advice originally, remember? I didn't know you were throwing a party.'

Dexter corrected him. 'Not a party. Just a few guys over from the set.'

'Some of the guys are wearing pretty neat bikinis,' Flint grinned. 'But before I go, Polly here wants to know what you've done with her bike.'

'What *I've* done with it!' Dexter looked blank.

Flint turned to the Chinese house-boy who was

arranging the hors d'oeuvres on a silver platter. 'Do you know what's happened to it, Wai? Did you chop it up and use it in those things?' He indicated the tray of piping-hot goodies.

Wai's grin nearly split his face in two. 'No, Mr. Flint. I not do that. Young lady's bicycle in garage behind car. These oyster patties not made with bicycles.' He giggled and held out the tray. 'Try one, Mr. Flint. They good.'

'I can guarantee that,' Sable reached out her slender hand for one of them, then nodded to Polly. 'Try one. They're great!'

But even though the flaky triangles made her mouth water, Polly was eager to get away. She shook her head determinedly, so that the thick braid down her back swung from side to side.

'No, thanks. I really must be going.'

But Dexter intervened. 'Aw, come on, sweetie! Try one,' he said, 'you'll hurt Wai's feelings if you don't.'

'Thank you.' Polly took one and bit into it. It was like biting into a buttered cloud, the filling both creamy and aromatic. The cook in Polly got the better of her reserve. 'This is *fabulous* !' she spluttered with her mouth full, 'I've never tasted anything so delicious.'

Wai grinned even wider and offered them all the tray again before leaving to distribute the appetisers among the guests outside.

'You've made his day,' Sable remarked. 'He's very proud of his cooking.'

Dexter was looking puzzled. 'What's eating you, Flint?'

'No doubt it's slipped your famous memory that you invited Polly for tea today. Tea, and an orgy of taped performances by Dexter Grant.'

Dexter asked Polly, 'Did I promise that?' and when she nodded shyly he looked at her as if she were the only person in the room and applied his well-known charm. 'Sweetie, I'm so sorry. I've just been so busy—will you ever forgive me?'

This, from her idol, melted all Polly's resentment. 'It doesn't matter—really . . .' she glowed, brushing a flake of pastry from her shirt.

'Really, Dexter!' Sable remonstrated. 'You are the *pits*! He does this frequently,' she explained, 'you mustn't take it personally.'

'I don't,' Polly assured her. She was now filled with happiness. She even forgave Flint for his interference.

'Nice performance, Dex!' The corners of Flint's mouth lifted sardonically. 'Now that's all settled I'll be on my way' He made for the door.

'Don't rush away, Flint,' said Sable, sipping delicately at her rum and orange, 'we've not seen you for *months*. It's not friendly to go tramping off all over India for months at a time, and then be unsociable when you come home.'

'It was Nepal, and it was only six weeks,' Flint grinned, 'but, okay, I'll stay for a bit. Do you still fancy a cup of tea?' he asked Polly. 'Because if you do I'll join you.' She nodded, and he went to the sink and filled the kettle.

In spite of herself Polly was intrigued. What on earch had Flint been doing in Nepal? It sounded so adventurous, and was a far cry from her first impression of him. She was about to ask him for details, when Dexter said loudly, 'You two can swill tea if you want, but *I'm* going to have another drink.'

'I'll get it for you, Dex,' Sable said, taking his glass, and Polly noticed that she poured in a very small amount of alcohol before topping it up with orange juice from a thermos jug.

'Thanks a *bundle*, Sable!' exclaimed Dexter. He reached across Sable to the bottle of rum and poured himself a generous tot in a fresh glass. There was a tense pause while the movie star took a deep swallow, smacked his lips appreciatively, then said to Polly, 'Do you work in our business, honey?'

'Nothing as exciting as that. I'm a typist—at least I

was. I'm looking for a job at the moment ' She felt dreadfully inadequate, admitting this, but Dexter hardly seemed to take it in She was beginning to notice that Dexter asked personal questions, but he wasn't really interested in the replies

Flint asked sharply, 'Are you any good?'

'I've not had any complaints,' she said

'You are looking for a job though?' He poured boiling water into a modern glass teapot and set it on the table 'What kind of work are you looking for?'

'I do temporary work. "Office Overload" jobs Typing mostly,' unconsciously she quoted her mother, 'while I sort out what to do with my life.'

Flint sat himself down opposite her. 'It is possible?' he said, looking at her speculatively. 'I wonder . . '

Polly's hackles rose. What did *that* mean? Did he query that fact that she might have a future? She glared across the table at him and said, 'It's my ambition to become a qualified cook.'

'Then why don't you?' asked Flint, pouring tea into two white mugs and passing one to Polly, 'if that's what you really want.'

'My mother doesn't want me to,' Polly confessed. Too late she realised that this sounded incredibly juvenile. Her normally pink cheeks flushed red. 'She doesn't think it's—well—good enough for me,' she explained, feeling disloyal to Marjorie now, as well as childish.

'You know, sweetie,' Dexter smiled over the rim of his glass, 'I've always been driven by ambition an' I gotta tell you something,' he finished his rum in one gulp and banged the glass dramatically on the table. 'You pay for ambition with your *blood*! I know—I've been there.' He smiled muzzily, satisfied that the conversation was again about himself.

'Talking of blood,' Flint remarked, '*National World Magazine* will have mine if I don't get my Nepal article in by the end of the month. Which brings us to *my* problem——'

'Havin' trouble writing it?' Dexter cut in nastily. 'It figures. I always thought it was a dumb move—you leavin' the fashion field.'

Flint didn't rise to the bait. 'My problem is merely technical,' he said. 'My one-finger typing is too clumsy and slow. I need someone to type and correct my manuscript if I'm to make my deadline in time.'

'You've got someone,' said Dexter. 'Some hairy Amazon who lives near you.'

'I'm sure Mrs. Jeffers would be thrilled by your description,' Flint smiled, 'but unfortunately she moved, with her equally hairy husband, to Halifax, so I'm really up the creek. I thought you might know of someone among your scintillating acquaintance who could type. That's why I dropped by today. I realise it's a wild chance, but I'm desperate.'

'Not so wild now that you've met Polly,' Sable pointed out. 'She can type *and* she's looking for a job.'

'Oh, I don't think I'd suit Flint!' said the horrified Polly. The very idea made her hair stand on end!

'Believe me, I'm desperate! I'm not looking for perfection,' Flint assured her ungallantly. 'And I'm willing to pay well.'

Polly looked daggers at him. Her eyes had turned dark gold with anger. 'It's not the money,' she spat. 'I don't think we'd suit each other ... temperamentally.'

'I agree that we don't seem to hit it off too well,' Flint said with maddening reasonableness, 'but it *is* only typing, and I need someone by tomorrow.' He gave her a crooked grin. 'I'm willing to control my nasty nature, if you'll do the same.'

She ignored this unexpected charm and said, 'Why don't you go to one of the agencies in town?'

'It would take too long. I've already told you, I need someone to start *tomorrow*.' In spite of his promise to control himself, there was an edge to his voice.

'You'd better meet that deadline on time, Flint,' Dexter said sharply. 'You're to start that photo-story of me at the beginning of next month. I don't want to put it off. I'm due to start rehearsals for that new play in England, and I want to take a vacation first.' He appealed to Polly. 'Why don't you say yes, sweetie? As a favour to me. I'd really appreciate it.'

'Don't beg her,' said Flint, his lips set in a grim line, but Polly paid him no heed. Dexter had asked her to do it as a favour to him, and as far as she was concerned that was enough. She was more than willing to put up with a few days' unpleasant working conditions for the sake of her hero. If she worked for Flint, surely it was possible that she would see Dexter again! It was worth a try at any rate.

'I'll do it,' she said, and allowed herself to smile across the table at Flint. 'After all, it's only a temporary job, we're not bonded for life.'

Flint, who was beginning to wish he had never mentioned needing a typist, looked at her glumly. 'I don't know,' he said 'on second thoughts, maybe it's not such a great idea. Do you have a car?' he asked, and when she shook her head he said, 'you see, I live in Caledon. It's too far to commute by bike. You'd have to move into the farm.'

'Well, what's wrong with that?' Dexter said, 'you've got plenty of room.'

But Flint still looked doubtful. 'What about your mother?' he asked. 'If she won't let you become a cook, how will she feel about this?'

'Well, Cakey's there, for heaven's sake,' said Sable. 'Mrs. Cakebread is Flint's live-in housekeeper,' she explained.

'For God's sake!' Dexter exploded. 'You've got plenty of action in that department without abducting Polly.'

Flint finally gave in. 'Well, I guess it's worth a try,' he said. 'If it doesn't work out we can call it quits and no hard feelings. Okay?'

'No hard feelings at all,' said Polly, but she wasn't really paying attention, her mind was still playing with that nugget of information Dexter had let slip, about Flint's sex life. He appeared to her so abrasive, she couldn't picture him as a lover, although there had been glimpses of charm. She supposed some women might be turned on by his lean body and craggy face, but as far as she was concerned there was no comparison between Flint McGregor and his dazzlingly handsome friend. Now if she had been going to move in with Dexter ...

There was a rumble of thunder from outside, and the sound of the first heavy drops of rain pattering against the leaves. They could hear the guests shrieking and laughing, and the door burst open and people tumbled into the kitchen like apples being poured from a barrel.

'My *dears* ! The heavens are about to open!' gushed a beautiful young man. 'The sky is *purple* ! I kid you not.' He smile brilliantly at this witticism and collapsed into a chair.

'I'll go and give Wai a hand bringing the bar indoors.' Flint got up from the table. 'Then I'll drive you home,' he said to Polly.

'But my bike!' Polly wailed.

'We'll put it in the back of my car. You can't cycle in this.'

He shouldered his way out of the kitchen. He was at least half a head taller than anyone else in the room. Not only that, he made them all look ... dull ... in spite of their fashionable gloss. There was a magnetic quality about him that she hadn't noticed before. She must have been crazy when she first met him to think he was a delivery man! Flint McGregor was no lackey delivering parcels. She was beginning to realise that he was a man to be reckoned with. She only hoped working for him wouldn't prove too awful.

With the transference of the party to the house Polly again seemed to become invisible. People surged around her, getting drinks, opening the refrigerator door to look for ice, and all the time talking at the tops of their voices. No one took the slightest notice of her, so she got up from

the table and stood by the big double sink, watching the
mob, overwhelmed again by a crippling sense of
inferiority.

After a while Flint came back. His shirt was wet, and
the rain water had soaked his coppery hair, turning it to a
dark roan red. At a glance he noticed Polly standing in
forlorn isolation by the sink and strode over to her.

'The car's waiting at the door,' he said. 'Let's make our
goodbyes and get out of here.' He put his hand under her
arm and started to guide her towards the door. 'Your's
bike's stowed in the back.'

'Did it fit in?'

'I had to buckle the wheel again, but I managed,' he
teased. 'We're off, Dex!' he called to the actor, who to
Polly's dejection was now draped over a particularly
luscious red head. 'See you around!'

'Sure thing, man . . . see ya!' It seemed to Polly that he
was having trouble focusing, but she quickly suppressed
such a disloyal thought.

'Do you want a lift any place, Sable?' Flint asked the
brunette beauty, who was regarding Dexter and his
curvaceous companion, a wooden expression on her
lovely face.

'I think I'll stick around here,' she said, 'thanks just the
same.'

Outside the rain came down, straight and silvery like
rods of steel. The orange BMW, its motor running, stood
waiting for them, a haven from the deluge.

'The doors are unlocked. Run for it,' Flint advised her,
and she did, but even so, the shoulders of her brown
blouse were streaked with rain, and her braid felt damp
on her back.

It was warm inside the car, and the windows were
misted over. Flint turned on the fan and pushed a tape
into the tape-deck. Neil Diamond's voice singing
'Suzanne By The River' filled the car. She gave him her
address and fell silent, listening to the music and
watching the rhythmic sweep of the windscreen wipers

as if hypnotised.

She now bitterly regretted her impulsive decision to take this job. There was no guarantee that because of it she would see Dexter Grant again. But she *would* see Flint. Living under his roof she would be forced to endure his sarcasm and the mockery in his blue eyes day after day. She must have been mad!

Had she known it, her future employer was having similar misgivings. I don't know if this kid can really type or not, Flint thought. She may turn out to be more of a hindrance than a help. How had he allowed himself to be talked into such a scheme? Panic, that's how, he acknowledged grimly, because it was a very slim chance that he would find anybody suitable by tomorrow. Panic—combined with a feeling of sympathy for this wacky girl. Solitary, pathetic even, but with a shy kind of dignity that threw him a little off balance. Well, dignity or not, he just hoped she was competent at her job!

It was still pouring when they drove up to Polly's house. Marjorie's Honda was standing in the drive. She was home! Polly leapt out of the BMW and wrenched the rear door open. 'I can manage,' she assured Flint, as she struggled with her bicycle, heedless of the rain that was soaking her hair and plastering her blouse to her full breasts. If she could just get her bike out of his car she could make a quick getaway and prevent him meeting her mother.

He switched off the engine and joined her in the rain. 'Don't be ridiculous. And stop pulling like that, you'll tear the upholstery.' He leaned in to ease the bike out. In seconds his back was drenched. She could see the play of muscles over his shoulders as clearly as if he were stripped to the waist, and for one wild moment she felt an urge to trace the line of his spine with her fingers.

She tried to take the bike from him, but he kept his hold on it and pushed it up the walk. 'Where do you keep it? In the garage?' She nodded, trotting behind him like an apprehensive kitten, one eye on the door for Marjorie.

He leaned the bike against the wall and peered out at the relentless downpour. 'Do you have such a thing in the house as a drier that I could use?' He plucked at his soaking shirt.

Courtesy forced her to invite him in. She could hardly let him drive to Caledon wet to the skin.

They went into the house by the back door, past the window-boxes of petunias that Polly tended so lovingly, into the little porch, painted white, where Polly had arranged garden chairs over an old rug she had bought at a garage sale. The dark sky made the usually cheerful room seem gloomy, and she switched on the lights.

'In here!' Marjorie called from the living room, and with a beating heart Polly padded in to her mother in her bare feet. Marjorie was sitting on the sofa, surrounded by papers, a full ashtray on the floor in front of her. The air was blue with smoke. 'Just sorting out the minutes for tomorrow's meeting.' Marjorie's eyes, hazel like her daughter's, narrowed. 'I thought you'd be wetter than that.'

'Yes, well, I got a lift. 'And Mr. McGregor is going to dry his shirt before driving home.'

'Who?' Her mother looked put out.

'Flint McGregor. He's—he's giving me a job, too . . . I don't have time to explain *now* . . . he's waiting in the kitchen, for heaven's sake. . .'

Marjorie rose to her feet, scattering papers and ashes. 'I don't know what you're talking about, Polly,' she said, 'I'd better meet this man,' and with a feeling of doom, Polly followed her.

Flint seemed quite at home. He stood barefoot and dripping on the tile floor, dwarfing the little kitchen with his considerable height. He had pulled his shirt loose from his slacks and unbuttoned it.

'This is very kind of you,' he smiled at Marjorie, who didn't smile back, 'I'm pretty wet. If I could just dry my shirt, I'll be on my way.'

Marjorie merely nodded sourly and hastily Polly

introduced Flint to her mother. 'Mr. McGregor drove me home from the—party. He said it was too wet for me to cycle,' she explained.

'What party?' Marjorie snapped, 'I didn't know anything about a party.'

'Neither did Polly,' Flint remarked soothingly. 'She came to pick up her bike, and found a theatrical party in full swing.'

'*Theatrical!*' Marjorie made it sound like an orgy. 'Are you an actor, then?'

'Not me. I'm a professional photographer. But my friend is an actor, and Polly's bike was in his garage.'

Polly butted in. 'Let me have your shirt,' she said. She was desperately anxious to get him dried off and out of the house.

Nonchalantly he rolled down his cuffs and slipped the blue garment off his shoulders. He was quite tanned for a redhead. A pleasant golden-brown, with a generous sprinkling of red-gold hair on his muscled chest. Polly began to understand why Dexter had implied that Flint had plenty of women ready to go to bed with him. He might not be conventionally handsome, but there was a rugged maleness about him that was undeniably attractive.

'What sort of photographer are you?' asked Marjorie, sitting down at the kitchen table and lighting the inevitable cigarette.

'A good one, I hope,' smiled Flint.

'Do sit down, Flint,' Polly said, glaring at her mother and offering him a chair. It was the first time she had addressed him by his Christian name. She did it deliberately, hoping it would somehow make Marjorie's rudeness less offensive. Not that Flint seemed at all put out. He sat back in the chair, as self-possessed as if he was in his own kitchen, fully dressed and surrounded by close friends.

'I've just finished my first photographic essay,' he told them. 'A documentary about Nepal. Before that I worked mostly in the fashion field.'

'*Fashion!*' If it had been hard-core pornography Marjorie couldn't have been more scathing. 'You mean you manipulated women into decking themselves out for the purposes of seduction! Fashion is a masculine trick designed to shackle women into the subordinate role for ever. It exploits and demeans women by encouraging them to catch a man, and then passively sit back and play the old stereotypes of wife and mother, without ever questioning their destiny.' She stopped for breath.

'That seems a bit sweeping,' Flint observed mildly. 'I merely found it rather dull. From a photographer's point of view, I'm really more interested in natural science than in the latest trends. So I switched. I'm also trying my hand at writing my own material to go along with the pictures. Which is why I've offered your daughter a job.'

He explained his predicament to Polly's stone-faced mother. 'There is one hitch, though,' he said. 'I live and work out of town, and Polly tells me she doesn't have a car. It would mean her moving to my place till the article's finished. My housekeeper, Mrs. Cakebread, lives on the premises, so Polly would have a—kind of chaperon around.' There was a glimmer of mischief in his brilliant eyes.

'Polly's nearly twenty years old. I don't tell her what she can do,' Marjorie said. Wryly Polly remembered her many battles about going to cookery school. 'Besides, she's taken karate lessons. She can look after herself.'

Flint raised his eyebrows. 'I'll remember that,' he murmured.

Unable to stand any more of this, Polly said, 'Your shirt should be dry enough by now,' and went over and pulled it out of the drier. It was still slightly damp, but she didn't care. All she wanted was to get him out of the house before Marjorie started on another of her shrill lectures.

He thanked her and pulled the shirt over his powerful

shoulders. She was again conscious of his flesh and the clean male scent of him.

Apparently satisfied that this masculine intruder was on his way, Marjorie doused her cigarette in the sink and headed back to the living-room, saying, 'If you'll excuse me, I've got *work* to do.'

'Of course, Mrs. Slater,'—he was as suave as if he was attending a diplomatic reception—'I'm glad we've had this chance to meet.'

Turning on the threshold she corrected him. 'It's Ms, not Mrs.'

'Of course,' he smiled pleasantly. 'Sorry.'

Marjorie nodded, her face set, and turned on her heel.

Scarlet with distress, Polly asked, 'Is it dry enough? Your shirt . . . Shall I put it back in the drier for a bit?' but she was relieved when he shook his head.

'Can you start really early tomorrow?' he asked, making for the back porch. I'm coming in early myself to take some shots of the waterfront at dawn,' he tilted his head towards the rain-drenched garden, 'as this should have cleared up by then. I'll pick you up and drive you back with me. Can you be ready to leave at six-thirty a.m.?'

'Sure!' Polly replied without a moment's hesitation, although six-thirty was rather a shock.

'We haven't discussed money, or is the pleasure of working for me payment enough?' He grinned, and Polly grinned back, grateful that he was making it easy for her to dismiss that embarrassing episode with Marjorie.

He named a sum. 'And you'll be getting room and board,' he pointed out. 'Is that okay?'

'Perfectly okay,' she agreed, a little dazed, since it was twice her usual salary.

'I'll see you tomorrow, then.' At the door he paused. 'Did you really take karate lessons?' he asked.

'Yes—but I wasn't very good.'

'I shouldn't think it was your style.'

Thinking he was referring to her weight, she flushed and asked, 'What do you mean?'

'The martial arts. You don't strike me as the combative type.'

'I can fight if I have to,' she told him, 'but I have to be provoked.'

'That makes sense. I only hope *I* don't provoke you.' He gave her that charming wry smile of his. 'I demand a lot from my typists, but up to now none of them have attacked me!'

'I'll try and control myself,' she said, surprised that she found it so easy to joke with this man whom she regarded as an adversary.

'Tomorrow morning, then,' said Flint, 'and don't be late. I don't want to hang about in town.'

Nettled, she assured him, 'I'll be waiting. Don't worry about it.'

'Oh, I won't! Calm your ruffled feathers. I just want to make sure.' Bye now, Polly . . . and thanks for drying my shirt.' He smiled briefly, and the next minute he was gone.

The kitchen seemed suddenly very empty, as if a powerful electric generator had been switched off and all the life had been drained out of the room. Which was stupid, Polly thought, because Flint meant nothing to her. But he had a way of getting under her skin, antagonising her one minute, and then doing something nice the next. She only hoped they could maintain the civilised truce they seemed to have achieved during the past half-hour. But frankly she doubted they would. And it was with a sense of foreboding about her new employer that she began to prepare supper for herself and Marjorie.

CHAPTER THREE

FLINT turned up on the stroke of six-thirty the next morning. Polly had been waiting since six a.m., determined not to be late by a single minute. However, since she didn't trust her alarm-clock, she had woken every hour to check the time, and was consequently sleepy and irritable.

Flint opened the trunk and threw the holdall in, on top of a jumble of tripods and other photographic equipment. 'Is this it?' he asked. 'No steamer trunks lurking in the bushes?'

'It's only for a few days,' she reminded him with some acidity, 'I don't need much.'

'Even so—none of the women I know have heard of the phrase "travel light". You should see the mountain of luggage Sable hauls around for weekends; one needs a moving van!'

Polly didn't comment. Sable's travelling habits were of no interest to her. Although she did wonder how Flint managed to be so well informed on the subject.

'Nice morning after all that rain,' Flint chatted. 'Or do you dislike sunshine?' he went on when she didn't answer.

'It's very nice,' she replied shortly.

'Well, I'm glad you approve,' he said cheerily. 'I trust you feel the same way about dogs.'

'*Dogs?*' she echoed, startled, and then she saw that the back seat was occupied by an enormous Old English Sheepdog.

'Meet Duvet,' said Flint. 'She's very friendly. Nothing to worry about.' As if to confirm this, Duvet waved her tail and regarded Polly through bright blackberry eyes.

Polly forgot her fatigue; dogs were a passion of hers. 'She's *lovely,*' she enthused, patting the dog's head. 'Aren't you, Duvet? You're a beautiful, beautiful dog.'

'Well, she certainly seems to have made you more agreeable,' Flint remarked. 'You looked about as friendly as an alligator with toothache just now. Now, Duvet, that's enough!' he ordered, for his dog, having found a friend, was enthusiastically licking Polly's face and hair in a riotous welcome. 'Now that you've calmed down, perhaps you could concentrate on making a list of the shots I'm going to take.'

She looked at him blankly. 'Shots? I thought we were driving out to Caledon.'

'We are. But I want to take a couple of shots at the C.N.E. grounds first. The sun wasn't right before. There's a clipboard and pencil back under Duvet somewhere.' He gestured with his head. 'I've made a list of the dawn pictures I took. All you have to do is add to that. It shouldn't be *too* difficult,' he added, rather nastily, Polly thought, when she hesitated.

She unbuckled her seat-belt and, kneeling on the seat, groped around under the large dog, who, thinking this was a new game, growled happily and tried to 'catch' her hands. 'The only difficult thing is trying to find this damn board,' she snapped. 'Why on earth don't you have some sort of system, instead of hurling things about like this?' She discovered the clipboard wedged in a corner and grabbed it. 'Duvet . . . *No!*' she yelled, as the ecstatic dog started pulling on the other end, shredding Flint's notes in the process. 'Let go! Bad girl, let go!'

Duvet relinquished her hold, and Polly slipped back into her seat. 'Wonderful!' she remarked. 'What she hasn't torn, she's slobbered over. Do you always file your notes like this?'

'I don't have time to think about filing them when I'm out on the field,' he replied. 'I'm much too busy observing things.'

Polly found his tone pompous, and instinctively she bristled. 'What sort of things?' she asked shortly.

'When you're a photographer you soon learn to be on the constant look-out for likely subjects. You train yourself to keep your eyes peeled—all the time!'

She raised her eyebrows laconically. 'I trust this vigilance doesn't interfere with your driving,' she murmured.

He looked at her briefly. 'You're a fine one to talk!

After your performance on that bicycle of yours I should keep quiet about other people's driving if I were you.'

Since she was unable to think of anything withering to say, she contented herself by giving him a wintry little nod, and turned her full attention to examining his hastily scrawled notes.

They proceeded this way in wary silence until Flint suddenly braked the car, so that Polly nearly went through the windscreen.

'What now?' she snapped, removing Duvet's large paws from where they had landed on her shoulders.

'Look at that!' Flint pointed to an early morning jogger, a young woman in brief shorts and sweatshirt. The thing that singled her out from the other joggers they had passed was the baby-carriage she was trundling in front of her as she ran.

'Marvellous! I've got to get a shot of that,' Flint exclaimed, and, stretching across her, he took a camera from the glove-compartment and wound down the window on her side. He steadied his arms on the edge of the lowered window, leaning heavily against Polly, while he focused his camera on the girl with the pram.

Polly sat as low in the seat as she could. His forearms were pushed against her breasts, and his lean, hard thigh was pressed tight against hers. She could see the glint of red-gold hair on his lightly tanned arms, the stubble on his jaw, a darker shade of copper than his hair, and his surprisingly long lashes. She could feel the warmth of him, and the rhythm of his breathing—and she was filled with the desire to press herself closer. Amazed by this attack of lust—for surely it could be nothing else—she tried to pull herself away.

'Stop moving around!' Flint barked, 'you'll ruin the shot.' Clearly his desires were solely photographic.

She froze with embarrassment and tried to will herself to ignore the contact between them.

The jogging mother rounded the corner, and, for the first time, Flint seemed aware of Polly trapped beneath

him. He eased himself back into his own seat. When he
did speak his voice was curt. 'You might make a note of
those shots.' He handed her the camera. 'I squeezed off
six frames.'

She did as she was bid. She was still trying to come to
terms with her own reaction to Flint's physical closeness.
While it was true that she was inexperienced sexually,
she had boyfriends and been kissed and held close, but
never before had she felt this almost primal urge to
respond so ardently to a man's touch. It was most
unsettling!

The sun was gaining strength, and downtown Toronto
glittered like a diamond. As they neared the lakeshore
she could see the railway tracks. 'Go Trains', looking like
green caterpillars, came into Union Station, and crowds
of early commuters streamed from them. The towering
skyscrapers turned the downtown streets into shadowy
canyons of glass and concrete, canyons that would
vibrate with heat as the day progressed.

They entered the Canadian National Exhibition
grounds—know to Toronto citizens as 'The Ex'—and
parked near the Princes' Gates. Flint hurried to the trunk
of the car and hauled out a large black bag which he
handed to Polly.

'Look lively,' he said, 'or the light I want will be gone!'

Polly glared at him. She couldn't understand how, only
five minutes ago, she had felt desire for this domineering
male. 'Is that your manuscript?' she enquired sweetly,
slinging the bag on to her shoulder. 'No, it's far too
heavy! It must be the typewriter.'

He was now wrestling a tripod out of the trunk. 'Stop
chattering,' he said. 'I need you to carry some equipment
for me if I'm to catch the light.'

He strode across to the base of the gates and tipped his
head back to scrutinise the statue on top of the arch.
'Lovely,' he murmured, 'the Angel of Progress herself!'

He reached into the bag Polly was holding and pulled
out a disreputable baseball cap which he jammed on his

head before taking out a camera, attaching a zoom-lens to it and fixing the whole thing on the tripod. Polly stood there, feeling about as important as a hat-stand.

Flint now became an extension of his camera. His concentration was focused on the angel on top of the gates, and for him nothing else existed.

Polly shifted the heavy bag to her other shoulder. She reflected bitterly that she had not been aware, when she accepted this job, that part of her duties would be to serve as a kind of ambulatory camera rack for Flint McGregor. But he was paying her a good salary, and as long as this didn't become a habit she supposed she wouldn't gain anything by complaining. She was just grateful that Marjorie couldn't see her now. That liberated lady would have had plenty to say about it!

Flint finished taking pictures from that angle, and after dismantling the camera handed it to Polly. 'Make a note of those shots,' he said briskly. 'Now for some different perspectives.' He picked up the tripod and walked away from the arched gates, with Polly trailing behind.

After dodging through the traffic, and narrowly escaping being run down by impatient motorists, they reached the opposite side of the road. Flint stayed in this location for some time, taking nearly a full roll of film. He wound up lying on his back to get the angle he wanted, and Polly began to understand why he dressed in shabby jeans and workshirt. She'd had no idea that taking pictures could be such a grimy business.

Finally he pulled his tall frame out of the gutter and studied the trees at the side of the road. He walked over to a tall chestnut.

'I'm going to climb up this one,' he informed Polly. 'I'll need you to station yourself in the lower branches so you can hand me equipment.'

Polly blinked up into the tree. 'The—the lower branches?' she faltered.

'Yeah! Put down the bag and I'll give you a hoist.' He

took the bag from her shoulder, then bent double. 'Use my back to get you started,' he directed.

Clumsily she scrambled on to his broad back, thanking God that she had worn slacks this morning. She clutched at the tree trunk and started to heave herself on to a fairly substantial branch.

'Hang on!' Flint said, and, straightening, he grasped her around the hips and pushed her unceremoniously into the tree. If she hadn't been scared stiff of climbing trees, she might have reacted to his firm hands on her. As it was she was barely conscious of his touch.

'Now pull yourself up higher,' he commanded. 'That branch above your head should do it.'

'Okay!' breathed Polly, feeling sick with apprehension. Even since she could remember she had been terrified of heights.

'Let me climb out of your way first,' said Flint, scrabbling in the bag for a camera which he hung around his neck.

'Okay!' Polly repeated like a hiccough.

He looked into her face. 'You all right?'

'Of course I am. Hurry up or you'll miss the light.' She would crash to the pavement and lie there, a crushed and bloodied mess, before she would admit her terror.

After he had started to climb, with as much assurance as if he were going up a solid staircase, she gritted her teeth and cautiously eased herself upright. She jammed her feet on to the branch and pressed her back against the trunk as if it could glue her to safety. There was a fine dew of perspiration on her forehead which had nothing to do with the heat of the sun. Her hair kept falling into her face, obscuring her vision and adding to her panic.

'This is great,' Flint shouted down to her, 'I can use some of the foliage as a frame.'

'Who cares!' said Polly under her breath. 'Just get on with it ... get on with it!'

The next few minutes stretched out like an eternity to her. Dumbly she handed equipment up to Flint.

Stretching up on her toes, her blood congealed with fear, never looking down in case she might fall. At last he declared that he had finished.

'I'll come down first and give you a hand,' he told her, slithering down the trunk and on to terra firma.

She handed him the bag and stood, rooted on her branch. Flint's face beneath her seemed to swim, as if it was under water.

'Come on!' he said, 'you can swing yourself down from the lower branches.

Carefully she slid herself into a sitting position, nearly lost her balance, then clung on for grim death, rigid with panic.

'Polly, are you all right?' Flint called.

'N . . . no,' she answered weakly, 'I don't seem t . . . to be able to move.'

'Hang on!' he said, 'I'll come and get you,' and in a moment his head and shoulders appeared on a level with hers. 'Now put your hands and feet where I tell you . . . and don't worry. I'm right beneath you. I won't let you fall.'

Quaking, she obeyed him. When she reached the lowest branch of all he slid to the ground and putting his strong hands around her waist he lifted her down and stood her on the blessed, firm earth.

Her legs felt like rubber and she was shaking. She tried to move out of his arms but he still held her close, and she trembled in his embrace.

Gently he stroked her hair. 'There, there! You're okay now.'

The trembling subsided and shame took its place. She pushed him away roughly.

'Why didn't you tell me?' he demanded. 'Why didn't you tell me you were frightened?'

'Because it's . . . *stupid*. That's why,' she choked.

'It's not stupid to be scared of heights. It's called acrophobia if my memory serves me.'

'If I *had* told you, you would have missed your light.

You wouldn't have liked that, would you?' she jeered.

'I hope I would have understood,' he said. 'Am I such a monster?'

'It's all very well for you,' she fumed, 'shinning up and down trees like a mountain goat. You don't know what it feels like—not being able to do things . . . '

'Goats don't climb trees,' he pointed out, 'and besides, you *did* climb the goddammed tree; and you didn't let on that you were petrified; all in all I'd say you were pretty courageous.'

'Courageous!' She stared at him, the wind taken out of her sails.

'Certainly, and you didn't drop any of my cameras. For that you get full marks! Now stop being an idiot and let's get some breakfast. I didn't have breakfast this morning, did you ?'

'Just an apple and a cup of coffee.'

'You see! You were probably faint from lack of food.' He rescued the tripod and slung the bag over his own shoulder this time. 'I know a place that make great bacon and eggs. Come on.'

Feeling much more cheerful, Polly followed him back to the car. She had been so sure he would despise her for her weakness. It was a great relief to discover that instead he understood her fears. Marjorie had repeatedly nagged her about it, and had tried to persuade her to stand on the extreme edge of the Scarborough Bluffs when they had picnicked there, even though the place was plastered with signs warning people not to go too close. 'You must overcome your timidity, Poll,' her mother had said. 'This is a man's world, and you have to become tough to survive in it.'

The restaurant Flint stopped at was unpretentious, but, as he had promised, the food was first class and the coffee delicious. When they had finished the bacon and eggs, they relaxed over a second cup.

'Feeling better?' he enquired, and when she nodded he said, 'you should have told me you were scared, Polly. I did wonder if you were okay at one point, but I get so wrapped up when I'm working I tend to become careless of other people.'

'It doesn't matter now,' she assured him. 'I'm on the ground again, and no harm done.' Had he known it, she was still savouring the word "courageous" in her mind. She would get pleasure from that for quite some time.

He stirred his coffee thoughtfully. 'You mustn't let yourself be bullied,' he said, 'there's no future in that.'

Polly traced patterns in the toast crumbs on her plate.

'You don't understand,' she said. 'I get so frustrated. I seem to be so ... so untalented. It would have been *another* admission of failure if I'd told you I was scared to climb that tree. I'd like to succeed in something,' she finished wistfully. 'Just once.'

'You have a burning ambition to climb trees?' he teased.

'I don't have a burning ambition to do *anything*.' She pushed the plate of crumbs away. 'It drives Mom insane.'

'What about the cooking school?' He took a sip of coffee. 'Aren't you ambitious about that?'

'Yes, of course I am! But that's ... well, it's easy. Oh, I don't mean I wouldn't work at it,' she went on in a rush, the way she did when she was trying to convince Marjorie. 'I'd work like *mad*. But I enjoy it ... I mean, it's sort of fun, so I guess you can't call it ambition. Besides, it isn't much to aspire to, is it? I mean, being a cook isn't very ... prestigious.'

Flint looked at her from lowered lids. 'What's prestige got to do with it ?' he asked.

'Well, if I had the talent to be a ... a nuclear physicist, or a ... a brain surgeon ... something like that. That would be something to be proud of, wouldn't it? But *cooking!* I mean, everybody can cook——.'

'I can't,' he cut in, 'nothing nourishing anyway.'

'But you could if you put your mind to it,' Polly insisted, carried away on the tide of her own unworthiness, 'anybody could. So it's not much of a career, is it? I mean it's pretty low on the achievement side of things.'

'Not very prestigious, in fact,' he said with disarming blandness.

She nodded miserably. 'Exactly! And the fact that I enjoy cooking, that I enjoy doing *all* demeaning domestic chores, just goes to prove that it isn't difficult. Otherwise I wouldn't be able to do it.'

'I never heard such *garbage* in my life,' Flint exploded. 'Do you really believe that enjoying what you do makes it worthless?'

'Well, no—but——'

'I thoroughly enjoy my work, and let me tell you I'm damn good at it. And as for your opinion of the career of a cook,' he glared at her furiously, 'that's nothing but snobbish rubbish. A good cook is just as important in our society as a nuclear physicist or a brain surgeon. You're insulting when you talk that way.'

'I don't mean to insult anyone.' She was stung by the scorn in his voice. 'But surely you'd agree that being a cook isn't exactly forging a path for the new woman in today's world. I'd just be ... ' she groped for one of Marjorie's phrases, 'perpetuating a stereotype about women. Shackling myself to the kitchen stove as some man's slave. I don't even want to run my own restaurant,' she confessed unhappily, 'that's how little ambition I've got.'

'Don't parrot other people's ideas, Polly,' said Flint. His temper, which had flared so suddenly, seemed to have died as quickly. 'It weakens your argument.'

'I don't want to argue. In fact, I don't know why we are.' She looked at him beseechingly. 'You don't need to get so angry.'

'I always get angry when I'm confronted with pretentiousness,' he informed her. 'It makes me mad. I was surrounded by it when I worked in fashion, I meet it head-on among Dexter's crowd ...'

'Dexter isn't pretentious,' said Polly, leaping to the defence of her hero.

'I didn't say he was. It's the people around him I find hard to take.'

'Sable doesn't strike me as being pretentious,' Polly went on doggedly. She didn't know why she was labouring this point, but Flint had caught her on the raw with his remark about parroting other people's ideas.

'Sable isn't really one of Dexter's crowd. Not in the sense I mean it.' He swallowed his last dregs of coffee. 'Let's drop it, shall we? We've got work to do, we can't sit here bickering all morning.'

He led the way to the cash desk, ignoring Polly's efforts to pay her share of the bill. 'You would have eaten breakfast at the farm, so it's part of your salary. Don't be tedious,' he said when she insisted.

With bad grace she gave in and followed him back to the car. Flint took a biscuit from the pocket of his jeans and gave it to Duvet who had been waiting patiently in the shade of a tree.

'Look at Duvet,' he said, scratching between her woolly ears. 'She doesn't have an ounce of ambition, but she doesn't get edgy about it. Do you, old girl?' Duvet wagged her tail and noisily sniffed his pockets for more biscuits. He pushed her away, laughing. 'Time to go home.' Duvet bounded towards the car, barking happily. Flint turned to Polly. 'And now, Pollyanna, let's head for the hills. We've got work to do.'

As they drove away Polly slumped disconsolately in her seat. Duvet might be thrilled to be going to the farm, but Polly was unable to share her enthusiasm.

'You have to do some serious work on your self-image, kid,' said Flint, throwing her a quick glance. 'You have a bad habit of selling yourself short.'

'I don't sell myself short,' she muttered defensively, 'I just wish I had better motivation, that's all.'

'Your motivation had better be honed and ready to have a go at my manuscript,' he replied, 'that deadline's starting to make me twitchy.'

'That's *typing*!' She was derisive. 'Typing's easy.'

'Not to me. Wait till you see the mess I've made of it.'

She didn't answer this. She knew she was upset out of all proportion, but Flint disturbed her. He brought things to the surface of her mind, things she thought she'd safely buried. She knew she had an inferiority complex. Well, so what? she reasoned, lots of people had. But she also knew she did nothing to make herself conquer it; she just sat back and passively accepted her own, and her mother's, bad opinion. And she suspected that this was what Flint found unacceptable. In her heart she did too, for she was not cowardly by nature.

They left the main highway and headed towards the Caledon Hills. Gentle, undulating country replaced the industrial sites. A shallow stream meandered alongside the road, and the lush valleys were dotted with farms and cattle. They drove through the quiet little town of Caledon—an overgrown village with a scattering of antique shops and one modest restaurant—and turned on to a gravel road.

Here the trees met over their heads and the pattern of leaves was like feathers against the sky. Duvet thrust her nose out of Polly's window to sniff at the scented air. A sign read, 'Hidden Driveway', and after a moment Flint made a sharp turn on to a long, tree-shaded dirt road. Polly just had time to read the white and gold painted notice that hung at the turning—'Crabtree Farm. A. McGregor'. They drove for quite a long time, it seemed to Polly, before climbing a small rise and coming to a halt outside the house.

Two things surprised her. The first was the farmhouse itself. She hadn't known what she had been expecting. Anything really, from a broken-down dump to a modern bungalow. What she was totally unprepared for was this graceful, charming old house, two stories high, built of beige stone, with dormer windows trimmed with glossy white paint. In the front of the house was an incredible expanse of green meadow that dipped and fell away from the flagstoned patio. The valley was criss-crossed by a stream, and dotted with apple trees.

The second surprise was the sight of Sable standing on the porch. She was dressed in a thin silk nightie and was eating yogurt out of a carton.

CHAPTER FOUR

'AH, Sable! You finally surfaced!' Flint opened the car's rear door and Duvet hurtled off into the meadow to chase imaginary intruders. 'And how do you feel this morning?'

'Not so bad,' Sable replied. She waved her spoon at Polly. 'Welcome to Liberty Hall!'

'Good morning.' Polly knew she sounded rather formal, but the truth was she was stunned to find Sable here, and in her nightie! Her last glimpse of her had been in Dexter's kitchen, when she had refused Flint's offer of a lift. Since then she had clearly changed her mind!

'Where's Cakey?' asked Flint, shouldering Polly's holdall and leading the way towards the house.

'She went into town to shop,' Sable told him, 'for garden supplies.'

'It figures.' He sounded grim. 'Has she done anything about food, do you know?'

'Search me! This is the last of the yogurt.' She held out the nearly empty container. A faint breeze caught at her pale oyster-coloured nightdress, so that it was moulded against her body. If I were built like that I'd wander around in next to nothing too, Polly thought enviously.

They entered the spacious hall which was decorated with creamy, rose-flecked wallpaper. All the woodwork had been painted white, and it gleamed in the sun which shone through a stained-glass fanlight, causing a pool of colour to shimmer on the highly polished floor. A hand-braided rug, woven in shades of cream, rose, and leaf green, added a touch of cosiness.

'Take Polly up to the guest room, will you, Sable?' Flint said. 'I'll go and check if Cakey's got anything in for dinner.'

'Should I phone the—the city—do you think?' Sable asked him pensively.

Flint's expression became enigmatic.'*I* wouldn't. But it's your life, Sable. You must do what you want.'

'I just get so restless in the country.' She smiled at Polly who was waiting at the bottom of the stairs. 'There's nothing to do, is there?'

Polly, who could think of a million things to do in the country, didn't answer.

'If you need a job,' said Flint, 'you can go grocery shopping. I'll bet my bottom dollar we're low on food.' He snapped his long fingers impatiently. 'Time is *passing*, girls!' he barked.

'Okay, okay!' Sable placated. She handed him the empty yogurt carton and the spoon. 'Take these into the kitchen, would you, Flint? If you're going that way.'

'Meet me in the kitchen in five minutes, Polly,' he said briskly.

'*Yessir!*' Polly answered, determined to make it in three. She picked up her holdall. 'Lead the way, Sable!' she commanded.

Polly's room was at the end of a long corridor, and faced an orchard—she could hear the gurgling sound of a brook which ran through it. She threw the nylon bag on to a pine rocker, and took a quick look round her domain. Everything was fresh and flouncy. There were blue forget-me-nots on the wallpaper, and blue ribbons looped back the starched, white cotton curtains. The bedspread was white too, with a scattering of primroses embroidered on it.

'You share a bathroom with Cakey,' Sable informed her. 'And with me when I'm here.'

'Are you here a lot?' Polly tried to sound casual, aware that it was really none of her business.

'Off and on,' was the vague answer. 'This place is a sort of bolt-hole.'

Polly wasn't quite sure what she meant by that. She wondered if Sable and Flint were lovers, although they seemed awfully casual together. Perhaps Sable meant that when she 'bolted' to Flint's house, she also bolted into his bed. For some reason the image of Flint as a free and easy lover was a distasteful one, and when she asked Sable where the kitchen was her voice was sharper than the question warranted.

'Just follow the hall downstairs to the back. You can't miss it. Don't you want to freshen up first?' Sable asked.

Polly grinned. 'No time! Simon Legree's waiting!'

'Oh, him!' Sable shrugged her slim shoulders. 'His bark's worse than his bite. Well, I guess I'll try to do something about my face, and go off to the store.'

'Your face is always lovely,' said Polly, but now that she looked closely she noticed that Sable's eyelids were red and swollen, and she wondered if the model was suffering from the effects of a hangover. You know, most women would kill to look like you.'

'Most women are much better off than I am, if they only knew.' Sable's face was a mask of gloom.

'You'd have difficulty convincing them of that,' Polly assured her. 'Now I've got to run. See you later,' and she sped out of the room, and down the wide staircase, taking an appreciative glance at the framed flower-prints hanging in the hall on her way.

Flint had just finished making a grocery list, which he put on one of the pine counters, together with a bundle of dollar bills. He gave Polly an approving look.

'Ah, you're here! Good. Follow me and let's get the show on the road!'

'What a *super* kitchen,' Polly remarked as she hurried after him. For, even though she had only been in it for a couple of seconds, she had had time to admire the long room that served both as kitchen and living-room, and which had a fireplace flanked by two cretonne-covered wing chairs at one end, and a vast amount of pine storage and work space at the other.

'I wish Cakey was as enthusiastic about it,' said Flint. 'Her interests stop at the back door.' He led the way down a back staircase, opened a door, and escorted Polly into a large office.

It was a functional room, but the white plastered walls were hung with many framed photographs—Flint's, she supposed—and a picture-window had been let in to the outer wall, giving a view of the tree-dotted valley, which relieved the severity.

'There's my manuscript,' Flint said. But all she could see was an electric typewriter that was almost hidden under sheaves of paper that spilled over a large desk, covering every square inch of space.

She picked up one of the sheets and eyed it sceptically. It was covered with deletions and additions in red ink. 'Did you at least number the pages?' she asked.

'Of course I did. But you can see why I need help, can't you?'

'You certainly need *something*,' she said severely. 'Perhaps a sense of order might be a step in the right direction.'

'It's the clerical stuff that defeats me,' he explained. 'I can manage everything but that.'

Polly took charge. 'I shall need filing folders, and paper in different colours, so we can colour-code each draft. Do you have those things?'

He indicated a metal cupboard at the side of the room. 'They should be in there,' he said meekly.

'Good! And it would help me if I could see some of the photographs you'll be using. So I can get a feel of what the visual part of the article will be.'

'Yeah, I can let you have those,' he agreed. 'Then, if you don't need me, I must shower and change before I attack all the work piled up in the darkroom.'

'I don't need you. I'm *tidying up,*' she said sternly, and with a grin he left her to it.

In spite of his assurances, Flint had *not* numbered every page, so this was a lengthier task than she had first anticipated. She was impressed with the content of the article however; Flint had an eloquent style, and his description of the people he had encountered in Nepal was vivid and alive.

She worked steadily for a couple of hours, hardly aware of her employer, who, having put a sheaf of photos on her desk, closeted himself behind one of the doors—the darkroom presumably—and didn't emerge again for some time.

She had just put the last page neatly in the folder in front of her, and was sweeping up the assortment of paper-clips and rubber bands that Flint had strewn over the desk, when he materialised in front of her, a tray in his hands, and Duvet at his heels.

'Time for a break,' he said. 'I've fixed us some lunch. Shall we have it outside?'

'Lunch!' She looked at her watch. 'Is it one already?'

He grinned at her. 'Time sure flies when you're having fun. Would you open the door? I can't manage it with this tray.'

She discovered the sliding glass door, and together they went out into the sunshine. Flint set the tray on the grass under a tree. 'Don't you touch!' he warned the sheepdog, who sat and gazed lovingly at a plate of sandwiches. 'Do you need a chair?' he asked her, 'or will you settle for the ground?'

'The ground is fine,' she said, sitting at the base of the tree and leaning against its smooth trunk. She wished now she had taken the time to change when she had taken her bag upstairs. Flint was freshly showered and shaved, and had exchanged his worn jeans and denim shirt for a pair of clean khaki trousers and a navy shirt. He smelled faintly of cologne, an aromatic scent she was beginning to recognise as his. She felt decidedly rumpled in her jeans and creased orange tee-shirt.

'There's beer or fresh lemonade,' said Flint, holding up

an old pressed-glass pitcher so that the ice-cubes clinked
'Or I could get you some milk.'

'Lemonade will be terrific, thanks.' Polly realised she
was very thirsty.

He poured some into a matching pressed-glass tumbler
that was rimmed in faded gold, and handed it to her.
'There are cheese sandwiches on brown bread, and ham
on white. I put mustard on the ham,' he warned.

'I *love* mustard.' She took a ham sandwich. 'My mother
would approve of this.'

'Approve of what? Mustard on ham sandwiches?'

'Idiot!' She took a bite of sandwich and said with her
mouth full, 'Of you getting the lunch, and serving it to the
hired help. Generally not behaving like a male chauvinist employer.'

'I take it your mama is quite a Women's Libber,' Flint
remarked, helping himself to a cheese sandwich and
giving Duvet a piece.

'Ardent,' Polly said. She took a sip of lemonade and
then balanced the glass between two tree-roots.

'Are you?'

'An ardent feminist?' He nodded. 'Well—not exactly.
Although I do support a lot of their ideals.

'So do I.' He took a large bite out of his sandwich.
She looked at him, surprised. 'Really?'

'*Really!*' he kidded. 'I should think any normally
intelligent person would agree that equal pay for equal
work, and equal opportunities for women, is only fair.'

'A surprising number don't. For instance, a lot of men
can't imagine working for a woman boss.'

'I worked for three years for a woman,' Flint said. 'She
was talented and tough, and I learnt more from her than I
ever did at college. No jewels will fall out of anyone's
crown because they make a cup of coffee.' He took a
swallow of beer and asked casually, 'How does your
father feel about it?'

She nibbled on a piece of ham before replying. 'I don't
have a father.'

'Is your mother a widow?'

'No' She looked past him at the far orchard that seemed to dream in the hot sun, like a mirage 'My mother's a single parent, she explained My father deserted her when when he found out she was going to have me'

She always hated talking about it Not that she was ashamed, but she dreaded the mixture of embarrassment and pity that flashed over people's faces when she told them the circumstances of her birth But Flint didn't look embarrassed Nor did he commiserate with her. He merely said, in a perfectly ordinary voice, 'That must have been pretty rough on your mother.'

Relieved that he was so matter-of-fact, Polly went on in a rush. 'Yes, it was. That's why I feel so badly that I haven't really turned out the way she wanted. She hoped I'd be talented. An ambitious woman of the future.' She gave him a wry smile. 'And I'm not like that at all.'

'No.' He finished his beer and watched her give her last crust to Duvet, who had been gazing at it with mesmeric intensity. 'Don't let her bully you,' he advised, pulling the dog away by her collar. 'She's a bottomless pit when it comes to food.' He offered Polly the plate of sandwiches. 'Come on! You're falling behind.'

'No, thanks—I really shouldn't.'

'Why shouldn't you? I made a ham and a cheese apiece.'

'Because of my figure.'

Flint put his empty beer can back on the tray and loooked at her affably. 'I think you have a very nice figure.'

'Don't try to be kind,' she said tightly 'I know the truth. I know I'll never be really slim like . . . like Sable.'

'Good God! Do you want to look like a model?' He seemed genuinely bewildered. 'Models are just clothes-horses, you know. Not a feminine curve among them.'

'But Sable always looks so . . . so elegant,' Polly protested.

'Sure she does. That's her style. You haven't found your style yet. Now, come on,' he held out the plate, 'eat your other sandwich before Duvet has a nervous breakdown.'

'My style is dowdy-fat. Nothing can be done about that,' Polly remarked gloomily, taking the proffered sandwich.

'For a sensible girl you do talk a lot of rubbish,' Flint said. 'I just presumed that you felt the way your mother does and that's why you look . . .' he hesitated, '—as if you couldn't care less about your appearance.'

'A mess, in fact,' she glowered, and, appetite vanished, she began to feed her sandwich to the dog.

'A bit of a mess,' he agreed cheerfully. 'But nothing that can't be easily fixed.'

Her first reaction was to take umbrage and retire into dignified silence, but she remembered that he had started the whole thing by telling her she had a nice figure, so she thought better of it and asked,

'How would I start?'

'Well,' he said, 'you could get your hair styled. You have a small face, and all that hair hanging over it makes you look like a relative of Duvet's.'

In spite of herself she smiled. 'Duvet's adorable,' she said.

'You could be, too, if we could *see* you.' Flint leaned forward and pushed his fingers through her fringe of curls, holding the silky tangle off her forehead and staring at her intently. 'You have eyes the colour of tortoiseshell,' he murmured. 'It's a crime to hide them.'

He was so close she could feel his breath warm on her cheek, see the texture of his lips. For a moment neither of them moved, then he released her hair and sat back.

In an attempt to break the erotic tension that had risen she said lightly, 'Maybe I should shave my head?' But he answered her brusquely, 'There's a good hairdresser in the village if you're interested.' And then he started asking questions about his manuscript, as if they had never had a personal conversation in the whole of their acquaintance.

She worked steadily until late afternoon. But by four o'clock the print started to swim before her eyes. She was putting the cover on the typewriter when Flint came out of his darkroom, and she offered to make them both a cup of tea.

She rooted around in the kitchen for mugs and tea-bags while the kettle heated, and opened a box of cookies she found in a paper-sack of groceries that Sable had presumably dumped on the counter. A large ginger cat, who had been sleeping on a window-sill, woke up at the rattle of crockery and proceeded to wind himself around her bare legs, purring like a buzz-saw, so she gave him a saucer of milk before taking a tray of tea and cookies down to Flint.

She took her mug of tea to her room where she unpacked her few clothes and toilet things. Her demin skirt and jeans looked lonely hanging in the enormous antique pine wardrobe.

It was very quiet. All she could hear was the chinking sound of a trowel in the garden, and when she looked out of her window she saw the dungareed behind of the gardener bent over the rows of vegetables.

Taking her sponge-bag, she went down the corridor to the bathroom she was to share with Sable, and Flint's housekeeper. A door to one of the bedrooms stood open and curiousty getting the better of her, she stepped inside. Flint's discarded jeans and shirt lay in a heap on the white pile carpet.

This must be his room; the master-bedroom. A king-size brass bed, covered in a teal-blue bedspread, stood against the far wall. A scarlet and white striped chair occupied a corner near a bookcase that was crammed to bursting. She had a glimpse of an adjoining bathroom tiled in grey and white, and she could smell the faint, aromatic scent of his aftershave.

Hastily, for she felt she was intruding, she backed out,

and, tripping over her trailing bathrobe, she stumbled against the door opposite Flint's room.

The latch gave and she was faced with a room that looked more like a women's boutique than a bedroom. Dresses hung over the cupboard door and were flung across the bed. Underwear festooned the dressing-table, and several pairs of high-heeled sandals lay negligently on the pastel pink rug. This must be Sable's domain. Closing the door hurriedly, Polly told herself that she had no reason to feel upset because it looked so permanently lived-in and was so close to Flint's room. For all she knew—or cared, she insisted to herself—Sable only used her bedroom as a dressing-room, and slept with her lover in that big brass bed.

She found the bathroom without further mishap. It was a large room dominated by an old-fashioned bath-tub that had feet like eagle's claws. Someone—Sable, maybe—had painted the nails with scarlet nail-varnish. There was a modern, glass-enclosed shower stall as well, and she decided to use that, since soaking in a tub was liable to send her to sleep after her long day's work.

There was plenty of hot water, so she had an extended scrub and washed her hair. When she was drying herself on one of the thick blue bath towels, she noticed an antique wash-stand against one wall. It was covered with bottles and lotions, cotton-wool, eyebrown pencils, lipsticks, and the general paraphernalia of a girl who models for a living. More of Sable's territory!

Polly reached for an electric hair-drier, and wondered why this further evidence of Sable's occupancy should cause her to feel a *frisson* of irritation.

Instead of waking her up, her shower seemed to have made her sleepier, so she pulled the bedspread back and stretched out on the bed for just a minute or two ...

She dreamed that a large woodpecker, the size of the ginger cat downstairs, was pecking at her door trying to get into her room and take it over. In a panic she blinked her eyes open, but the pecking continued.

'Polly!' Sable called, tapping harder. 'Polly, are you in there?'

'Come in.' She sat up groggily as Sable poked her head round the door. 'Wha . . . what time is it?'

'Nearly six. Flint and I are going to have a pre-dinner drink. Will you join us?'

'Yes, sure—I'll just put something on,' Polly said, sitting up. Hurriedly she turned her back on Sable who had come into the room, for she was painfully aware that she was only wearing her bra and panties, and she felt that the contrast between her lush body and Sable's thinness was more than she could bear.

'What lovely skin you've got,' Sable remarked on her way to the dressing table to check her eye make-up in the mirror. 'What body lotion do you use?'

'I d . . . don't use anything. Just soap and water.' Polly was so startled by this unlooked-for compliment that she forgot to be shy.

'You lucky thing,' said Sable, delicately smoothing at her eye-shadow with her little finger, 'most girls would kill for skin like yours.' Satisfied that the shadow was now properly blended, she turned and gave Polly a stunning smile. 'And it's not just your face. You've got flawless skin all over.'

Polly looked down at her creamy breasts that curved so voluptuously, at her smooth tummy and rounded thighs. She had always taken her pearly complexion for granted; it was a revelation to discover it was an asset that could be envied by other females. Especially females as glamorous as Sable.

'Now get a wiggle on,' Sable chivvied her, 'I'm dying for a drink.'

Since she didn't have much choice it only took Polly a few seconds to pull on her denim skirt and a crimson and brown check shirt. 'I'll just comb my hair,' she said, 'and I'll be with you.'

This proved to be easier said than done. Sleeping on her damp hair had hopelessly tangled it. With her eyes full of tears of pain she tugged at the comb until finally she threw it on the dressing-table in disgust. 'Sorry, Sable,' she said, 'I'll have to tie it back and make the best of it.'

'We can do better than that,' Sable replied. 'Is that the only brush you have?' She indicated Polly's worn soft bristle one and Polly nodded. 'Let's go to my room,' said the lissom model, leading the way. 'I have a steel comb that should deal with the problem.'

She opened the door of her bedroom. It *was* the room opposite Flint's, Polly noted glumly. Sable wielded the comb and started combing, and in a surprisingly short time Polly's matted curls were free of tangles.

'What *have* you done to the front of it?' Sable asked, fingering Polly's bangs critically.

'I tried to cut it myself . . . with a pair of nail-scissors,' Polly admitted. 'I wanted a change.'

'Well, you got that all right!' She pulled the thick fringe to one side and secured it away from Polly's face with a hairpin. 'Ever worn your hair up?' she asked. Polly shook her head. 'Let's try it, shall we? It won't take a minute, and I think it would suit you.'

Without waiting for an answer she deftly lifted Polly's mane, and with a few quick movements pinned the weighty mass on top of her head. 'There! Take a look in the mirror and tell me what you think.'

The mirror reflected back a Victorian maiden with a delicate face, topped by a wealth of shiny brown curls. 'Oh!' breathed Polly, as she smoothed the upsweep of hair with her palms. 'Oh, it looks super!'

'It's your style all right.' Sable sounded pleased with herself. 'You've got such strong hair, all you really need is a good haircut and a couple of combs, and you're in business. Now, let's go and get that drink—I'm gasping!'

They joined Flint on the front patio where he was sitting with a tray of drinks in front of him. Polly kept catching glimpses of herself in the windows. Her new hairstyle made her face look thinner, and she had to discipline herself not to keep peeping at her reflection all the time in wonder. She waited for Flint to say something, but he didn't. Although he did give her a piercing glance when they first joined him.

It was a beautiful evening, and after Flint had poured the girls a Dubonnet on ice they sat back in grey-painted cane chairs and silently watched a family of barn swallows give a brilliant display of aeronautical skill.

No one spoke. Each of them was wrapped in his or her own thoughts. Sable's seemed to make her restless, for she fidgeted against the yellow cushions, and tapped her fingers on her glass.

Polly sat still, enjoying the feel of the soft breeze playing with tendrils of hair that had pulled free and lay lightly on her neck. The swallows dipped and tumbled against the backdrop of evening-tinted sky, and the fragrance of grass, and earth, and flowers filled her with content.

After some time spent in this silence Sable asked when dinner was likely to be ready. 'Because if it's going to be delayed I might just ring the city,' she said.

Flint roused himself. 'Bad strategy,' he advised. 'As for dinner—the last time I asked, it was some time after eight.'

Sable reached for his wrist to look at the watch strapped to it. For some reason this intimate gesture gave Polly a quick stab of . . . of what? Jealousy? But that was rubbish. Why on earth should she feel jealous of Sable and Flint?

'Dinner's a whole hour away,' said Sable. 'I think I *will* ring,' and she got up and stood by the open door.

Flint said, 'Suit yourself. But you'd be much better off coming for a walk instead.' But Sable merely smiled and went into the house. 'Well, *I'm* going for a walk,' he said. He rose and looked down at Polly. 'Do you want to come? Or would you rather sit here and listen to your stomach rumble?'

'My stomach isn't rumbling,' Polly replied, 'but I

wouldn't mind seeing a bit of the farm before it gets dark.'

Flint scooped up a handful of peanuts and then held out the bowl. 'Better take a ration of those,' he advised. 'When Cakey says any time after eight, it could mean midnight.'

She took a handful, saying, 'I'm not really hungry,' and followed him to the back of the house. Duvet, who had been lying on the back porch, got up shook herself, and then trotted behind Flint's heels.

They passed a fence-enclosed garden, which was neatly weeded and smelt of freshly turned earth. Flint gave the plot of vegetables a look of intense indignation. 'My gardener hasn't been near the place for weeks,' he growled, without warning.

'But I saw him . . . well, I saw someone, working in the garden this afternoon.'

'You saw my housekeeper,' Flint replied bitterly. 'Cakey would rather garden than *breathe*—as I discovered to my cost after I'd hired her.'

'Oh!' Polly grinned to herself. So *that* was what had been occupying him for the past half-hour—irritation with his housekeeper! 'Why don't you get someoene else?' she asked.

He glared at her in exasperation. 'Because—A, I don't have the time to interview people. And—B, it's not as easy as you might think to get someone to come out here, away from the discos and the bright lights. Crabtree Farm isn't the most desirable place to work, it seems.'

'Really?' She was genuinely surprised. 'I think it's a heavenly place!'

Some of the anger died in his blue eyes, and he said, 'I think so too. But it can be lonely. Especially since I'm away quite a bit of the time.'

'But there's Duvet . . . and the cat . . .'

'Ah, you've met Fellini, have you?'

'Mmm! I love ginger cats.' She increased her pace to keep up with his long-legged stride. 'And I don't see how anybody can be really lonely in the country. Besides, it's less than an hour to Toronto, isn't it?'

'Remind me to have you around for P.R. work when I interview a new housekeeper.' He smiled wearily. 'Because it's quite clear that Cakey will have to be replaced.' The smile vanished and he went on, as if to himself, 'And it couldn't come at a worse time. First the Nepal article to finish, and then the photo-story of Dexter.'

With a twinge of something like conscience, Polly realised that, until Flint had mentioned his name, she had not given a thought to Dexter Grant all day. To make up for this oversight, she asked, 'Have you known Dexter long?'

'Since we were kids. We were at boarding school together.'

'Did he want to be an actor when he was at school?' She had a romantic image of Dexter, handsome even as a child, confiding his secret dream to his carrot-headed friend.

'He didn't let on,' said Flint. 'Neither of us thought much about the future in those days. It was hard enough coping with the present.'

This sounded very mysterious, and she said, 'I don't understand.'

Flint's mouth set in a hard line. 'We were both very unhappy at boarding school,' he said tightly. 'It's not always the happiest place for little boys.'

'That's awful,' she said, her maternal heart touched. 'Did your parents know you were unhappy?'

'Dexter is the product of several sets of parents,' Flint explained dourly. 'I doubt they would have known.'

'Poor Dexter!' She was wrung with pity. Then, in order to be polite, she added, 'And what about you? Do you come from a broken home, too?'

He gave a bark of harsh laughter. 'Oh, no! My parents are very securely married—to each other *and* to their work.'

'Their work?'

'They're both doctors,' Flint said shortly. 'They work together in a teaching hospital.'

'Your mother's a doctor, too?' Polly asked, impressed.

'One of the best,' said Flint, taking two giant strides in order to get to the top of a small knoll.

Polly trotted up after him. 'Do you mind not walking quite so fast?' she entreated. 'I have a hard time keeping up.'

He didn't reply, but stood motionless on the top of the little mound, looking at the distant hills, with unseeing eyes. Polly stood beside him. She would have liked to have commented on the view, which was particularly lovely in the setting sun, but Flint's mood was so forbidding she thought it prudent to remain silent.

Flint was twenty years away. Back in that school, a homesick nine-year-old, whose chief aim in life was to hide his misery, and never to be caught crying. Dexter, another neglected child, had come to the school a year after Flint, and their mutual loneliness had forged bonds of friendship that had withstood the years and differences of temperament.

He had come to terms with his parents now, but the nine-year-old Flint had been bewildered by their lack of interest, and he still found it difficult to forgive the countless school sports days, and parents' days, when the headmaster had relayed the inevitable phone-call from one or the other of his busy parents, explaining that the pressure of work made it impossible for either of them to attend. He remembered all too vividly the school holidays spent alone in his parents' apartment, trying not to get in the way of yet another new housekeeper who clearly was irritated at having a small boy underfoot.

He never spoke of those days. This was the first time in years he had allowed himself to dwell on them, and he was appalled that a casual question from this inquisitive girl had opened a wound he had thought was healed.

All at once he spoke, breaking the oppressive silence.

'I want a wife who's willing to invest her life in our home, not a career. And if I can't find a wife like that I'll stay single.' He did not raise his voice, but this statement had the force of a shout in its concentrated fury.

Polly stared up at him in total astonishment. She had no idea what could have provoked such an outburst. One moment they had been talking about his friendship with Dexter, and the next he was bellowing out his requirements for a wife! She could only suppose that he had had some kind of falling-out with Sable. Maybe the affair— for she was sure by now that they were lovers—was drifting towards marriage and Sable was reluctant; or had refused to give up her career. Whatever it was, it had plunged him into a miserable mood. He stood on the knoll, the gold light of the setting sun making his hair flame, accentuating the harsh lines on his face, so that he seemed older and utterly remote. A lonely figure comtemplating the horizon.

He became aware of the scrutiny and turned away abruptly. 'Better be getting back. It'll be dark soon,' he said as he marched off towards the house.

This time Polly made no attempt to keep up. She reasoned that, if he wasn't going to be sociable, to hell with him. If he wanted to indulge in an attack of the sulks, let him indulge by himself. She would walk at her own pace and admire the last trace of blood-red sun as it sank from view. It was only the idea that it might by bats, and not birds, swooping so close to her head, that finally made her quicken her steps.

He was sitting on the back-porch, Duvet beside him. 'I thought you might have decided to walk back to Toronto,' he smiled as she drew near, and from the teasing note in his voice she knew that his black humour had passed. But she did not feel inclined to cater to his swift changes of mood, and she merely replied shortly, 'I wanted to admire the sunset.'

She made for the door, but before she reached it he was on his feet beside her. 'Your hair looks very pretty like that, Pollyanna,' he said. He opened the back door and together they went into the kitchen. 'All you need now is some sort of soft dress, and you'll look perfect.'

Trust him to spoil the compliment, she thought. Now she was painfully aware of how wrong her mannish blouse and skirt looked!

Flint introduced her to his housekeeper who was slicing lettuce at the sink. Mrs. Cakebread, a raw-boned woman with a great deal of Flint's garden still under his finger-nails, nodded dourly to Polly, and then suggested they go and watch television until dinner time. 'It won't be long now,' she promised.

'Want to bet?' Flint said, just loud enough for her to hear.

'I'm going as fast as I can,' Cakey glared at him, but it had no effect on Flint, who said firmly,

'I'm delighted to hear it. We would like to get to our beds before midnight. Come along, Polly!' He held the door and led her from the room.

In the den Sable was curled up on one of the faded chintz sofas watching a thriller on television. She looked as if she had been crying. Flint sat down beside her and put his arm over the back of the cushions.

'Bad news from the big city?' he asked.

'No news at all.' She smiled at him wanly. 'Nobody's home.'

'Ah!' He patted her shoulder.

'And not expected to be. I mean—it could be *days*.' Her voice cracked and she concentrated furiously on the flickering screen.

Presently Cakey thrust her head round the door to announce that the meal was ready, and they trooped into the dining-room.

Polly hadn't seen this room before. It was papered in dark red and the ceiling and woodwork were painted a brilliant white. The large oval table was polished mahogany. A silver bowl, badly tarnished, and containing one withered apple, stood in the centre. More silver stood on the handsome old mahogany sideboard. Cakey had flung some plastic place-mats on the table, together with an assortment of kitchen cutlery, which jarred with the simple elegance of the room.

Grimly Flint sat himself down in front of a roast chicken, and, picking up a knife, started to carve it. Blood spurted from the bird and splattered on the table. With a roar of fury he threw the knife down and, picking up the platter of nearly raw fowl, made for the kitchen at top speed.

'Come on,' said Sable, in hot pursuit, 'this should be fun!'

Polly was not sure she would describe watching Flint rail at his housekeeper as *fun,* but it was certainly awe-inspiring. Despite his passionate indignation he never once paused for breath, or repeated himself. Even the stolid Cakey looked shaken. At the end of his recital of her many failings he cast the offending chicken on to the kitchen counter.

'Why you ever decided to become a housekeeper in the first place beats me!' he snapped. 'You certainly don't have the temperament for it.'

'I've been meaning to speak to you about that,' the woman retorted sullenly. 'I've accepted a job at the Caledon Nurseries. They need new help.'

Flint stared at her. '*Accepted* a job! What about the little matter of giving me notice first?'

'I'm giving you notice now,' Cakey informed him. 'Two days. I start work day after tomorrow.'

Polly held her breath, waiting for the storm to break. But there was no storm. Flint said, almost chattily,

'You don't have to wait two days to start your new job, Mrs Cakebread. If you come down to the office with me now, I'll write you a cheque to cover the time you've—gardened—this month. Then you can start your new job tomorrow.'

Suits me! I'm sure I don't enjoy cooking for your fancy women morning, noon and night!'

Flint turned on her, his lips a thin line. 'The ladies you refer to are guests under my roof,' he rasped. 'Since you choose to gratuitously insult my guests you are no longer welcome here. You will pack your bags and leave my house *tonight!*'

Swiftly he went down the stairs, followed by the now silent woman.

'Wow!' said Sable, when they had disappeared. 'I always knew she didn't like me, but she hardly fed me morning, noon and night!'

Polly smiled weakly. She wasn't sure she enjoyed being referred to as one of Flint's fancy women, even by such an unreliable source as Mrs Cakebread. To cover her discomfiture she replaced the chicken on its platter and wiped the surface of the counter with a cloth.

Flint came back upstairs, followed by a scowling Mrs Cakebread, who left them without a backward glance.

He looked straight into Polly's wide eyes. 'I'm sorry, Pollyanna. You didn't deserve that scene. And you must be starving.' He straightened his long back. 'I'll get the car out and we'll drive into Toronto for dinner.'

'Toronto!' Sable looked down at her pink jeans. 'I'll have to change, then. Why don't we go and eat in the village?'

'Because the restaurant there closes at nine, and it's ten-thirty,' he replied wearily.

Polly was galvanised into action. 'We don't need to go out for dinner,' she said. 'I can fix us a meal.'

She took a wedge of cheese and some olives from the refrigerator. 'Flint, you find some biscuits, or some bread, and we can have a snack while I figure out what to do with this chicken,' she ordered him. 'And Sable, would you bring me the dish of vegetables and the salad from the dining-room.' She smiled, her face alight with pleasure. This was the kind of challenge she enjoyed! She didn't have a moment's doubt that she could salvage the meal in double quick time, nor that it would be a good one.

Flint foraged in one of the cupboards and produced a tin of biscuits. 'Here we are, Pollyanna! And I think we'll open a bottle of decent wine. I've got some Chablis on ice. Let's celebrate the departure of Mrs Cakebread from my life.'

They set the table in the kitchen for this second attempt at dinner. Flint cut squares of cheese and put them on a pretty glass plate with the olives, and they all munched contentedly while Polly cut up the chicken and sliced onions, before stir-frying their supper in a wok that Flint had found hidden behind a plastic bag of potting-soil. He served the pale straw-coloured wine in tall crystal glasses. It tasted to Polly like iced sunshine. Cold on the palate, but warming to the soul.

She started to stir the chicken in the hot oil when Flint offered her the cheese plate again, but she shook her head. Several glossy curls fell round her flushed face. 'Can't manage it,' she explained, 'I need both hands for this.'

'Here then,' said Flint, 'open up!' and he took a cube of Tilset and popped it in her mouth. The tips of his fingers brushed against her soft lips for a moment and she felt a delicious kind of prickling sensation under her skin. She jerked away with a mumbled 'thank you', for she didn't want him to touch her, no matter how innocently, if it was going to have that effect. He was Sable's man, and she wasn't interested. Adding a tin of pineapple chunks to the chicken, and stirring soy sauce into the pan, she licked her lips in an attempt to brush away the lingering memory of his touch.

She served the stir-fry straight from the wok on to old china plates whose rims were decorated with marigolds. Flint topped up their glasses, and spooned out rice that Polly had boiled from a packet she had discovered on the counter. She had made a fresh salad too, to replace the limp one they had been offered earlier, using a dressing of soy sauce and oil, for she knew it had an astringency that was just right with any kind of Chinese food.

Flint tasted a morsel of chicken, then formally raised his glass in a toast. 'To you, Pollyanna,' he said. 'You've not only saved the day but you've saved it magnificently.' She tried to reply, but he added, 'And if you say it's easy I'll belt you!' so she just grinned and sipped her wine.

They ate in silence for a while, being much too hungry to make conversation. For Polly the evening had developed a gala air, and she didn't think it was entirely due to the Chablis. Cooking and serving a meal to Flint, seeing him obviously relishing her food, made her ridiculously happy. Between mouthfuls she smiled contently, secure in the knowledge that she had done well.

'It is good,' said Sable with her mouth full. 'You're very clever, Polly. Cakey couldn't have made anything like this, not if her life depended on it!'

'How long has she worked for you?' Polly asked. She had just noticed that the fork she was using was an antique silver one. When Flint had set the table he had dumped the kitchen stuff back in the drawer and produced this cutlery instead.

'Not very long.' He speared a piece of lettuce and ate it. 'Your salad's terrific too,' he remarked pathetically. 'I needed someone just before I went to Nepal. The people who usually look after Duvet and Fellini were away, and I didn't want to board them, so getting a housekeeper seemed the best solution. It would leave me time to work on my article—I *thought*! I didn't know then that Cakey was going to behave like Capability Brown!'

'Well, you won't have to put up with her much longer,' Sable informed him. 'I heard her phoning for a taxi when I was in the dining-room.'

'I shall not weep tears of sorrow,' Flint remarked drily. 'I can't help feeling Cakey and I will be happier apart. But,' his brow creased momentarily, 'it couldn't have happened at a more inconvenient time. Never mind! I'll worry about it tomorrow ... Now, Pollyanna, shall I make coffee? Or have you dreamed up some luscious dessert?'

Polly started to collect the empty plates, but he took them from her, so she headed back to the refrigerator to get the dish of fresh strawberries she had doused in fine sugar, orange juice, and mint leaves.

They lingered over coffee and dessert, and after Flint had helped Cakey take her luggage to the taxi, which had arrived while they were still drinking their first cup, he celebrated their "liberation" as he called it, by pouring them all a liqueur. The alcohol, combined with her early morning, began to catch up with Polly, and she started to yawn uncontrollably.

'Bed, young lady!' Flint ordered, swirling the brandy around in his glass.

'But I want to do the dishes,' yawned Polly.

'No way, kiddo! You'd need toothpicks to prop your eyes open. Sable and I will do the washing-up. Won't we, Sable?'

Sable nodded. 'Sure we will,' she said uncertainly.

Polly glanced briefly at Sable's long red nails. 'It won't take a moment. Really,' she volunteered, pretty convinced that Sable didn't know one end of a dish-mop from the other.

But Flint was not to be overruled. 'Don't argue, Pollyanna,' he said, coming over and pulling her to her feet. 'I want to have a talk with Sable and we can do it over the dishwasher.'

Of course! thought Polly, I am dim! Sable had been crying when we got in from our walk, and she's his girl, and naturally he wants to find out if everything's all right between them. And she suddenly felt that they were no longer three comrades, but two lovers and one extra person. She was in the way. So she said without further protest,

'Okay ... I'll say goodnight then,' and climbed the shallow stairs up to her room.

As she undressed she told herself that she was wearier

then she had realised. Otherwise, why should she feel so—excluded—because Flint and his lady wanted time alone together? It was perfectly normal that they should want to be by themselves. She quite understood.

But when she heard the murmur of their voices beneath her window, and, peeping out, saw Flint's tall form stooped over Sable, his arm around her shoulders, she was filled with an inexplicable sadness. A sadness that filtered into her sleep, filling her dreams with loneliness.

CHAPTER FIVE

SHE woke early, and at first she didn't know where she was, then the white curtains fluttered, revealing a glimpse of the orchard, and the past events flooded back.

Her bedside clock said six-thirty, and she groaned. Was this early waking going to become a habit? But she was awake now, so she might as well get up. Hastily she dressed in her jeans and tee-shirt, and, carrying her sandals, crept barefoot down to the kitchen.

Duvet looked up from a basket in the corner of the room and thumped her tail on the floor in welcome. Crouching down beside her, Polly stroked her between the ears. The dog felt nice and warm, for it was overcast this morning, and the air in the kitchen was chill. She had put the kettle on, and found herself a mug and a tea-bag, and was just poking about in the bread-bin, when Flint said, 'Good morning!' from the doorway, so that she nearly dropped the bread knife on her foot.

'Lord help us!' she exclaimed, her hand on her breast. 'Don't creep up on people like that!'

'Sorry, but I don't want to wake Sable. She doesn't take kindly to early mornings.'

'Neither do I.' She wondered if Sable was curled up in

his big brass bed. Not that it made a jot of difference to Polly whose bed she was in. 'Do you want tea?' she asked, pouring hot water on to her tea-bag.

'I'll make myself coffee, thanks.' He took a filter from the cupboard and fitted it into the cone. 'Sure you wouldn't rather have coffee?'

'I simply prefer tea first thing,' she informed him primly, not feeling up to cheerful banter at such an ungodly hour.

Flint went to the back door to let Duvet out, and gazed up at the sky before coming back to the kitchen. 'Hope it clears by this afternoon. I had planned to take the plane up later.'

'*Plane!*' She stopped in the act of putting a piece of bread into the toaster.

'It's only a little single-engine job—not Concorde. I use it for work, mainly, but it's fun too. I'll take you up for a spin one day,' he promised, and she shuddered faintly, remembering the chestnut tree.

'What's the matter? Cold?' he asked. 'Don't you have a sweater?'

She admitted that she had not thought to bring one with her. 'Here, then! Have this.' He handed her the sweatshirt that was flung across his shoulders. It was faded grey cotton with a fleecy lining; warm and cosy.

'Thank you,' Polly said gravely, rolling up the sleeves which were far too long.

When the toast was ready they took it to the kitchen table and ate in companionable silence, then, after pouring himself a second cup of coffee, Flint said.

'I've been doing some thinking, Polly, and I have a proposition to make.' Polly stared at him over the rim of her mug, her tawny eyes huge in the dim morning light. 'To put it briefly, I was wondering if you'd like Cakey's job?' he said. 'On a temporary basis, of course.'

'What about your manuscript? Don't you want me to go on typing that?' She wasn't quite sure if she was being fired from one job, or promoted to another.

'Well, I was wondering if you could manage both. Two part-time jobs, so to speak.'

'That manuscript of yours is more than a part-time job,' she remarked grimly.

'Well, yes ... But you did such a splendid job with dinner last night. And I thought if I managed lunch ... and we helped ourselves to breakfast ... maybe you could manage dinner. It wouldn't have to be anything elaborate. We'll have to work something out about shopping for food, but I'm sure if we all pitched in it could work. What do you say? I'll pay you extra, of course.'

'We could give it a try,' she agreed. The thought of cooking a meal didn't phase her, and the extra money would be useful. And—Polly's heart rose—maybe Flint would invite Dexter for dinner one night. 'Yes,' she repeated, 'we could give it a try.'

'Fine! That's settled, then. I'll phone my cleaning lady later on and offer her job back, so all you'll have to worry about is the cooking.'

'I didn't know you had a cleaning lady,' said Polly.

'I didn't for a while. Cakey told her to get lost. Mabel—my "help"—likes to bring her grandson along, and Cakey didn't like children around.' He looked at her sharply. 'You don't mind them, do you?'

'I love children,' she assured him.

'There is one thing we must do before it's finally settled, though,' said Flint. 'You must tell your mother. She should know that things have changed since you first came to work here.'

'Honestly, Flint!' Polly stopped on the stairs behind him and he turned round. 'Sometimes you behave as if we were living in the *Dark Ages!*'

He set his lips stubbornly. 'Nevertheless, I must insist!'

Grumbling under her breath, she followed him into the office. She still thought he was being unreasonable, but part of her respected his stubborn integrity. She had to admit it was a good characteristic, and one she secretly admired. Glancing at her watch, she said,

'I should be able to catch Mom before she leaves for work. Will that satisfy you?' And he inclined his head with mock solemnity.

'You could mention that Sable is staying on,' he said. 'It might put her mind at rest.'

'Mom's mind is never at rest,' Polly snapped. 'And if she knew it was Sable who was the model for that suntan advertisement she'd be down here in double quick time with her can of spray paint at the ready!' Flint looked mystified, and Polly explained about Marjorie's vendetta on sexist advertising.

'Poor old Sable!' he grinned. 'In that case we'd better keep her identity to ourselves.'

'What price honesty *now?*' Polly said nastily. Ever since Flint had told her that Sable would be staying on at the farm she had felt annoyed with him. Which was silly because she liked Sable, and it was fun to have another woman around for company. What she couldn't figure out was why Flint and Sable didn't live together openly. Or get married, so that people would know where they stood.

She dialled her home number; after several rings Marjorie answered and Polly spent a frustrating five minutes explaining the new set-up. As she had foreseen, her mother wasn't concerned about the lack of chaperonage. It was the news that her daughter would be cooking, and cooking for a *man*, that infuriated Marjorie, and after a heated conversation, conducted by Polly in agonised whispers, she hung up.

'That's settled, then,' she said to Flint, who had tactfully turned his back to examine the contents of a filing cabinet during this exchange.

'You must ask your mother down for a meal some time, Polly,' he suggested. 'Or any of your friends if it comes to that. After all, all work and no play makes for a dull life.' That lovely smile of his lit his craggy face, and Polly's heart gave a lurch, but all she said was,

'I doubt if I'll be in residence long enough to organise anything like that,' and she started putting paper into the typewriter.

It rained during the morning, but by the time she took a break to make them both a cup of coffee the sky was starting to lighten and streaks of blue appeared between the clouds. She removed Flint's sweatshirt and hung it over a kitchen chair. She felt a mild regret when she did this, rather as if she had released herself from a comforting embrace, and she let her fingers linger for a moment on the faded material, reluctant to finally let it go.

Sable, wearing her silk nightie, staggered into the kitchen. 'I thought I smelt coffee,' she yawned, 'I sure could use some.' She glowered at the dripping trees that were now touched by a faint watery sun. 'What foul weather! I think I'll drive into town later. Escape all the mud.' She gave an elaborate shiver and, casually taking Flint's sweatshirt, pulled it over her sleek head, settling the waistband round her thin haunches.

Polly stared at her and for a moment, brief as a flash of lightning, she felt a wave of such possessiveness for the shabby garment sweep over her that she nearly cried aloud. She had loved the warm fluffy feeling of that shirt of Flint's against her own skin, and she didn't want to share it with Sable. She shook her curly head to dislodge such idiotic thoughts. 'Coffee's ready,' she said gruffly, then, clearing her throat, added, 'shall I make you some toast?'

'No, thanks. Too fattening.' Sable reached into the fridge. 'I'll just have some yogurt.'

Flint clattered up the stairs to join them. He greeted Sable warmly and planted a kiss on her forehead. 'Is that all you're going to eat?' he asked, and when she said it was, he said, 'you really should eat more Sable. Put some flesh on your bones.'

'And never work as a model again. For a fashion

photographer, Flint has some very weird tastes,' she confided to Polly.

'Nothing weird about liking shapely women,' Flint said, and Polly thought how disparate he and Sable were. Apart from sex, she wondered what the attraction between them could be.

'I'd give my eye teeth to be thin and *flat!*' she burst out impulsively, turning bright pink once she realised what she had said.

'Better hang on to your teeth, Pollyanna,' Flint advised her. 'I don't think there's much chance of that happening,' and she thought she heard him say, 'Thank God!' under his breath, but couldn't be sure.

'We're going to need some food if I'm to produce a meal tonight,' Polly pointed out to Flint.

'That means I'll have to take the time to go shopping,' he said irritably. 'And I'd planned to leave right after lunch for Toronto.'

'I can do it,' said Polly. 'This afternoon. It'll make a break from typing.'

'You need a car to get to Orangeville where we shop,' Flint told her. 'Unless you plan to thumb a lift each way—which I can't allow.'

Before Polly could give vent to her indignation, Sable interjected, 'Look, Flint, I want to go into the city too! Why don't you drive me in your car, then Polly can have mine for the shopping. It's manual transmision, is that all right?' she asked Polly.

'Perfectly all right,' Polly assured her with dignity. She pointedly ignored Flint.

'That's settled, then,' he said, draining his mug of coffee. As he made for the office he flung over his shoulder, 'Just try not to smash up Sable's car *before* you get the groceries.'

'Don't let him get to you,' Sable advised as Polly slammed her empty mug into the sink, nearly cracking it in the process. 'He loves to needle people.'

'I really am a good driver,' Polly said 'I won't mess up your car.'

'I know. So does he. Otherwise he wouldn't let you do it.'

'*Let* me! bristled Polly.

Sable sighed patiently. 'You know what I mean. He wouldn't want to risk your being hurt. You're far too valuable to him.'

After lunch, which Flint prepared, he and Sable drove off, promising to be back by seven. Polly took the money he had left her for shopping, and went to the barn that served as a garage. Sable's sporty little automobile stood in the gloom looking very smart and stylish. Gingerly, Polly put the key in the ignition and started the motor. She had decided to take a short drive first to get the feel of the car. She had also decided against taking Duvet with her. She was now sulking in her basket.

Polly drove around the country roads for about half an hour. She was still annoyed by Flint's teasing, for she knew she was a good driver. Cautious, but not so careful that she was a menace to other traffic. But she had not had her licence for many years, and this zippy little car was a far cry from Marjorie's battered Honda, so she didn't let her attention wander. She did daydream after a while, however, that this was her car, and that she lived permanently in the country, and was now going in to do her weekly shopping before returning to the farm that she shared with a loving husband. A husband who bore a remarkable resemblance to Dexter Grant. Several shadowy children were also included in this daydream, all of them miniature copies of their father.

She found her way to Orangeville without difficulty, and did her shopping, and after buying herself a new paperback and a bar of peppermint chocolate she headed for home.

She had just finished unpacking the groceries and was wondering if she should make a cup of tea before returning to the typewriter, when a sleek grey coupé came to a halt by the back door. Polly, followed by a barking Duvet, went to investigate. Then her heart gave a thump, for Dexter Grant got out, smoothed his immaculate blazer, and said,

'Hi, sweetie! Flint around?'

The colour flooded into Polly's face at this unexpected encounter. She told him Flint was out, and he received this information with a colourful expletive.

'I should have phoned first,' he explained, 'but I only got the afternoon off at the last moment, and I thought it would be neat to get out of town for a bit.' He kicked at the gravel with his highly polished shoe and swore again.

Polly told him that she had just been going to make a cup of tea, and invited him to join her. He looked at her unenthusiastically.

'Tea—no, thanks—but I wouldn't say no to a vodka and tonic. It's a long drive back into town.'

She wasn't sure that, under the circumstances, a vodka and tonic was a good idea, but she murmured, 'Of course,' and led the way into the house.

Dexter pointed at Duvet who was following them. 'Would you mind leaving the pooch outside?' he asked. 'I have an allergy to dogs.'

Polly dragged the reluctant dog back to the door and firmly shut her out. 'What sort of allergy?' she enquired.

'I dunno,' he said vaguely. 'They leave hairs on my clothes.'

'She's a super dog, though,' Polly persisted, willing Dexter to share some of her tastes.

'If you like dogs,' he agreed. 'Frankly, I go along with W.C.Fields. Dogs and children are death for actors.'

'Do you feel the same way about cats?' she asked, for Fellini had materialised and had started to weave himself in and out of Dexter's legs like an orange darning-needle.

'Pretty well,' admitted the actor, pushing the cat away

with his well-shod foot. 'Animals just aren't my bag, I guess.'

She found the vodka, and the actor helped himself to a pretty hefty slug of it. Polly had some of the tonic instead of tea. She now felt embarrassed about offering tea in the first place, since he apparently found it a very unexciting beverage.

'Do you want to sit on the patio?' she asked him, but he declined, and instead they sat in the sitting-room that faced the valley. Dexter seemed quite at ease, but Polly felt more and more unsure of herself and had to control the urge to fidget.

'Flint sure does live in an out-of-the-way spot,' Dexter remarked, gazing across the sunlit meadows. 'It must be hell in the winter.'

'Oh, do you think so?' She was disappointed, since she had already imagined Crabtree Farm shrouded in snow and decided it must be a perfect place to be. 'Don't you like the country, Dexter?'

'Let's just say I like to be where the action is,' Dexter said. You should see my new condominium in L.A. I had this really well-known decorator fix it up. It's very futuristic. The decor's in silver and white with glass and chrome, and push-button controls for all the doors. And a full-size movie screen! Talk about class!' He took a large swallow of vodka.

Polly privately thought it sounded like a hospital operating room, but she just said, 'Sounds wonderful!' and buried her tip-tilted nose in her glass of tonic.

There was an awkward pause. 'What time did you say Flint would be back?' Dexter asked finally.

'About seven, he said. Would you like to stay for dinner?' she suggested. Maybe she would feel more at ease with this glamorous creature if she could show off her culinary skills.

He finished his drink and rose from the armchair. 'Thanks, but no can do, sweetie,' he said 'I've got a hot date with a little redhead and I mustn't keep her waiting.'

Polly forced herself to smile at this.

'I wanted to tell Flint that there's going to be a big shindig out at the island the Sunday after next. It's being thrown by the film company, a publicity gimmick. The press'll be there. It's a kinda giant picnic, and I thought Flint might like to take some shots for the story he's going to be doing on me. Some pictures of me interacting with the public—signing autographs—stuff like that!'

'I'll tell him,' said Polly.

'You come too,' Dexter suggested, and she felt a stab of pleasure because he had included her. Then he spoilt it by saying, 'It's open to the public. The more the merrier.'

'Well—I'll see. I'm not sure where I'll be then.' Back home looking for a job most likely, she thought grimly. She would have finished Flint's manuscript long before that.

She walked with Dexter to his car and waved as he roared off down the drive, the gravel spraying out from under his wheels. Duvet trotted up to her and pushed her wet nose against Polly's hand which had stopped cheerfully waving and now hung listlessly at her side. She bent and encircled the dog in her arms, leaning her cheek against its woolly head.

'I'm sure he doesn't really dislike dogs,' she assured her canine companion. 'He just doesn't know how super you are.'

Duvet tried to lick her face in agreement, and then followed her back into the house to supervise the preparations for dinner.

There wasn't a lot to do. They were having steak with baked potatoes and a green salad. She made some banana custard, and sliced a couple of fresh mangoes into a glass dish to have something on hand if banana custard wasn't acceptable. Then, on impulse, she decided to make a cold cucumber soup. There was time, and she could chill it in the freezer.

All the while she became more and more depressed. This chance meeting with her idol had left her feeling at odds with herself and the rest of the world. She was painfully aware that not only did Dexter hardly remember her name, he didn't see her as a female at all! And who could blame him? she thought, looking down at her short jean-clad legs and sturdy sandals. But she had a nasty feeling that even if she were the epitome of glamour, all long legs and gorgeous clothes, the dissimilarity of their tastes would not change.

She fed the dog, then, deliberately unwrapping her chocolate bar, she devoured it slowly. She usually indulged her chocolate habit when she was feeling down. After her bath she tried putting her hair up, but she wasn't as successful at it as Sable had been—it looked a bit lopsided—so she took it all down again, and brushed it till it crackled, then she tied it back with a ribbon. As an act of defiance she put her jeans on again instead of the wrap skirt. When Flint and Sable arrived she was sitting on the steps of the patio looking out at the valley, wrapped in a mood of savage unhappiness.

'I got some good shots from the plane this afternoon,' Flint said when they had joined Polly for a pre-dinner Cinzano. 'I'll give you the list and you can make a note of them in the journal after dinner, Polly.' She nodded curtly. He looked at her sharply. 'What's the matter? Did you have trouble with the car?'

She looked daggers at him. 'No trouble at all, thank you.' Then, thinking she had better put forward some sort of explanation for her cranky mood, she said, 'I didn't get as much work done on the manuscript as I hoped. I had an unexpected visitor this afternoon,' and she gave Flint Dexter's message.

Sable, who had suddenly turned pale, said, 'It's too bad we missed him. He could have stayed for dinner.'

'He couldn't,' Polly said shortly. 'He had to get back for a date—with a redhead.'

Sable said 'Oh!' and then excused herself. 'I've got time for a bath before we eat, haven't I?' she said, and, leaving her drink unfinished, she hurried into the house.

Flint looked after her thoughtfully, then he turned to Polly. 'When did you say this picnic takes place? A week Sunday? It should be fun.'

'I don't care whether it's fun or not,' she said tartly. 'I'm much too busy to concern myself with it.'

'You'll have finished the article by then, won't you? Don't get in a flap.'

'I'll be finished in a couple of *days*,' she said, 'and I'm not in a flap.'

'Well, *something's* wrong,' he insisted. 'Your usual sunny aura seems to have fused.'

'I don't want to go to the damn picnic!' she snapped, and then blinked rapidly to keep the angry tears at bay.

'That's too bad,' he said. 'I was relying on you to help me with the story on Dexter. I was going to suggest you take on the job of my assistant for that one.'

She should have felt a surge of triumph when he said that, for, after all, her sole reason for accepting his job had been in order to get to know Dexter better. But for some reason Flint's offer made her feel even more dejected. 'I don't know if I could stand all the glamour. I don't think I'd measure up.'

'Measure up? Measure up to *what*, for God's sake?' he asked testily.

'Well—you all look so marvellous—and you're all so sure of yourselves . . .' Unable to express her feelings of insecurity adequately, Polly blurted, 'Even your *names* are glamorous. I mean . . . Flint! . . . Sable!'

'Sable's real name is Enid Pike,' he told her drily, 'and if you let on that I've told you I'll deny it. As for Flint— that's a nickname I got at school because I spent one whole year collecting arrow-heads—and because I *loathe* my given name.' She looked at him expectantly. 'I was christened Angus, and I warn you not to say anything about bulls!' She gave a weak giggle. 'Well, at least it raised a smile.'

'But you just don't understand,' said Polly, trying to make her position clearer. 'Whenever I'm with Dexter I feel so—so *nothing*. He's used to gorgeous women around him, and I feel so—ordinary. I don't know if I could bear to work with you on that story. You and Sable—you're part of that scene, but I'm not. I'd be miserable.'

He stood up, looming over her. 'You are so dumb sometimes, Polly, that I could hit you,' he told her. 'Being part of that world just takes a good haircut and a couple of fashionable outfits. It doesn't take any particular talent. But go ahead! Be my guest—if that's what you want out of life.'

'It's all very well for you!' She was starting to lose hr temper. 'You've been part of that world for ages; you can afford to reject it. But I've never had the chance. I'd like to experience a bit of glamour myself before I decide whether I like it or not.'

He stared at her intently. Her face was pale apart from two bright spots of colour on each round cheek, and her eyes glowed golden. He said wryly, 'Point taken, Polly,' then he leaned over her. 'I'll make a deal with you. Once the Nepal article is out of the way I'll make you over. We'll get your hair styled, and go into Toronto and get you a new wardrobe. I guarantee that when I've finished you'll feel as glamorous as the next woman.' He paused. 'I'll do this on the understanding that you'll stay on here and help me with the story on Dexter. Is it a bargain?' He held out his hand.

After a moment she took it. His flesh felt warm and dry against her palm, and she didn't mind when he did not immediately release her, but held her hand fast in his.

In her mind's eye she could visualise a door opening on to a glittering world. A world where she could operate with confidence. A world that contained Dexter Grant. She felt a wave of gratitude towards Flint who had promised to open that door for her. He really is a friend after all, she reflected, and then she checked herself, remembering that he wanted something in return. He needed her help with that story. They were just bartering favours.

She removed her hand from his clasp and thought that he seemed reluctant to relinquish his hold. Upstairs she could hear Sable moving about, so she said, 'I'd better start on those steaks,' and left him, not noticing his sombre expression as he stood in the gathering twilight.

In three days Polly had finished the article and made the acquaintance of Mabel, Flint's cleaning lady, and her small grandson, Neil. Neil was a serious child who at first spent some time gravely studying Polly and then decided that her sole purpose in life was to play with him. This she did on every coffee break, and during a good deal of her lunch hour.

Flint included himself in these pleasant sessions, but Sable made it quite clear that small children held no charms for her, and absented herself from the area of the play-pen.

Polly had found the courage to suggest several changes to Flint's article, which, she was convinced, would improve it, and to her delight he adopted them without comment. When they had gone together to the village Post Office to send the manuscript off, he had turned to her and told her that her help had been invaluable. 'I couldn't have done it without you, Pollyanna,' he had said, and she had turned pink with pleasure because she knew he was not a man who gave compliments easily.

He tucked the registration slip into his wallet. 'Now for the Polly Slater transformation,' he said, and instead of guiding her back to the car, he led her to a shop which had a pink and white striped awning over the window. 'Ila's Beauty Box' was painted on the door.

A petite strawberry-blonde wearing dark pink pedal-pushers and a champagne crocheted top came towards them. 'Flint!' she trilled, 'you're on time, bless you! I wish all my clients were as punctual.'

She had big blue eyes and a dazzling smile, and she was clearly very pleased to have this redheaded giant in her tiny salon.

Flint pushed Polly forward and introduced her. 'This is Polly Slater, Ila,' he said. 'She needs a new look, and I'm confident that you're the one to give it to her. Ila's the most talented stylist in all of Ontario.' he added in an aside to Polly. 'You can trust her absolutely.' Polly nodded dumbly. She had had no idea they were going to start her metamorphosis quite so soon, and now that it was happening she felt rather nervous.

Ila gave her a clinical stare, felt the texture of her nut-brown hair, and said, 'Come back in two hours, Flint. We'll be finished by then.'

Feeling far from confident, Polly was shown to a cubicle where she removed her wrap-skirt and tee-shirt and put on a pink gown. Then her hair was shampooed and her head wound up in a pink towel while she waited for Ila. The girl had not addressed one word to her personally, and Polly felt rather apprehensive. But after a brief exchange, when it was established that Polly's relationship with Flint was a working one, Ila thawed and Polly relaxed.

The pretty hairdresser took her time, studying Polly's face and bone structure carefully. Then, after a great deal of snipping and combing, Polly's hair was blow-dried and she was handed a mirror. The change was miraculous! Her hair now fell in feathery layers to her shoulders, the disastrous bangs had been trimmed and were brushed back off her brow so that her delicate face was softly framed in glossy waves. Her eyes now looked enormous.

'It'll be very easy to keep,' Ila promised. 'You won't even need to blow-dry it, and it's still long enough to put up. Do you like it?'

Experimentally Polly shook her head and her gleaming hair swung in a perfumed curtain, then fell back into shape again. 'You're a genius,' she told Ila. 'A sheer genius!'

Back in the cubicle she got dressed again. Now the brick-coloured tee-shirt looked *really* dreadful! She had noticed a rack of soft cotton dresses hanging in the reception area of the beauty parlour when they had come in. They were the work of a local batik artist, and now Polly went to investigate.

She chose a low-necked dress which was tied at the waist with a sash and fell almost to her ankles in soft unpressed pleats. It was patterned in shades of almond green and honey. She pushed the elasticised sleeves above her elbows and looked critically into the narrow mirror in the cubicle. She looked terrific, and although the dress showed more bosom than she was used to, she had to admit it was a vast improvement over her usual clothes. Delighted with herself, she went to the front desk to pay.

She was a bit put out when Ila told her that the hair-do had already been paid for by Flint, for she liked to feel independent, but she kept quiet about it and sat down to read a magazine until he arrived.

She was immersed in an article about eye make-up when the chimes sounded and Flint burst into the salon. For a second neither of them spoke, then he exclaimed, 'Polly! My God! You look beautiful!'

She stood up, collecting the brown paper bag containing her old clothes. 'It's not very polite to sound so surprised,' she smiled. She had the distinct impression that Flint was at a loss for words, while she felt in complete control, and she was enjoying the sensation.

He was still gazing at her. 'Your hair—it's terrific, Pollyanna—just terrific,' he said.

'It certainly beats my own cut,' she agreed lightly, but her heart was pounding pleasurably because he made her feel desirable, and this was heady stuff!

In the car she asked him what she owed him for her new coiffure. 'Nothing,' he said, 'it's a bonus,' and when she protested he explained that the bonus was for the extra work she had contributed to the article. 'Without your help it wouldn't have been half as good,' he said.

Since she was learning not to belittle her achievements

she thanked him and refrained from making any comments about it being 'easy'!

'By the way,' he said, 'while you were at Ila's I went to the bank so I can pay you your salary in cash, and run to an advance if you need it—for tomorrow's shopping.'

'I won't need an advance,' she told him, recollecting the money-order from her grandmother. 'I have some birthday money to spend.'

'When was the birthday?'

'It wasn't. I mean, it's in a couple of weeks.'

'And you'll be twenty, is that right?' He turned to look at her and his eyes lingered appraisingly for a moment at the shadowed cleft of her cleavage. She felt a tide of colour sweep over her chest up to her face. 'So young,' he muttered under his breath, 'and so damn vulnerable it hurts.'

Unable to hear him properly, she asked, 'What?' but he didn't reply, and since her new-found confidence had deserted her under the audacity of his gaze, the remainder of the drive passed in silence.

Sable was on the phone when they went into the house. She waved her beautifully manicured fingers at them and went on writing on a jotter. 'Fine!' Polly heard her say, 'sounds fine. Will nine o'clock be too late?' She mouthed 'Work' at them and gestured to the phone. With a grin she said, 'See you later, then!' and hung up.

'My agent wants me to come in to Toronto,' she said, and her dark eyes glittered with excitement. 'Some clients are looking for a model to publicise a new line of cosmetics and my agent's having dinner with them tonight. She wants me to join them.' She started for the stairs. 'I'll just have time to put on the war-paint and iron my dress. Sorry I won't be here for dinner, Polly. Hope it doesn't put you out too much.'

Polly assured her that it didn't, and then suggested that she iron the dress while Sable got ready. 'You won't mind waiting for your meal, will you, Flint?' she enquired.

'No problem,' he replied. 'I'm not hungry. I'll take

Duvet for a walk. Good luck with the job, Sable.'

He sounded so subdued that Polly wondered if Sable's obvious delight at this chance to rush off and pursue her career was upsetting him. If so it didn't seem to bother Sable, who led the way upstairs, unbuttoning her silk blouse as she went.

'You are an angel, Polly,' she chattered, 'this account is a very big one and includes a trip to Paris for promotional work—*if* I get it!' They had reached her room by now and Sable was pulling out dresses from the wardrobe and flinging them on to the bed. Finally she made her choice.

'*This* one, I think.' She held it against herself. It was a black silk shift—very short, and very narrow at the hem. 'It just needs a touch-up with the iron.' She looked at Polly closely for the first time. 'Your *hair,* Polly! It looks *sensational*! And I love your dress! I should have noticed before, I am a selfish pig.'

Polly smiled. 'No, you're not, you're just excited about this job. Now, you get to work on the face while I deal with the wrapping.'

It took only minutes to iron the dress, and when she brought it back Sable called, 'In here, Polly!' She was sitting in front of her dressing-table mirror in the bathroom, painting her face. She was clad in a pair of gauzy black tights sprinkled with silver moons and stars—and nothing else. The air was heavy with the musky perfume she always wore in the evenings.

'How do I look?' She turned towards Polly, who stood in the doorway. She was clearly nervous, and Polly had said in all honesty that she looked terrific. The black dress was the latest fashion, the black stockings with their silver motifs provocative, and the carefully made-up face had the mask-like perfection of a top *Vogue* model.

'Bless you,' Sable had said, fiddling with the single rhinestone ear-ring that hung nearly to her shoulder. 'By the way, Polly, if there's any of my make-up that you want to use, help yourself.' Polly had looked at her

blankly. 'For your tête-à-tête with Flint!' And she had
blown a kiss and flown from the room.

Tête-à-tête with Flint! Polly had to admit she hadn't
thought of it that way, and now that she did she wasn't
sure she liked it. Something about the intimacy of that
phrase frightened her. Of course, she reasoned, Sable
didn't mean anything by it, it was just a joke. Even
sophisticated fashion models surely didn't make presents
of their lovers for the evening.

But she was tempted to try some of Sable's eye make-
up just the same!

She put aside the thick salmon steaks that she had
already braised in a fumet of red wine. She would glaze
them in the oven and make the Genevoise sauce when
Flint returned from his walk. Right now she was going to
work on her eyes!

Fifteen minutes later, after a fascinating time experi-
menting with Sable's various pencils and shadows, she
came back downstairs. She had tried to remember the
tips she had read that afternoon in the salon. Her eyelids
were coloured with bronze shadow, and her long lashes
were spiky with mascara.

Flint was in the hall, carrying a tray with a bottle of
Cinzano and two glasses on it. 'I've fed the dog,' he said.
'Fellini must be out catching his own dinner, there's no
sign of him.' In spite of the ordinariness of these remarks
the atmosphere between them seemed uneasy. 'I thought
we might have a drink on the patio.'

She said, 'Its rather late. Maybe I'll have my drink in
the kitchen while I cook our dinner,' but he muttered
something about there being no rush, she had time for
one drink before she started cooking, so she followed him
outside.

When he handed her her drink he looked straight into
her face, and did a slight double-take. Polly lowered her
eyes, and her heavily made-up lashes fluttered like a fan.
Kicking off her sandals, she curled up in her cane chair
and continued to stare at the glass in her hand, very

aware of his scrutiny.

'Did Sable do your eyes?' he asked finally.

'No, I did,'—she looked up into his impassive face. 'Why? Is it wrong?'

'Not wrong exactly—but a bit heavy, Pollyanna.' Swiftly he came and knelt before her, whipping a handkerchief out of his pocket and touching a corner of it to his tongue. 'Hold still!' He gently wiped at the bronze shadow. 'There—that's better.' He sat back on his heels. 'The colour's right for you, but don't use quite such a heavy hand. And the same goes for the mascara. And extend the shadow out to the side of your eyes like this.' He touched the corner of each hazel eye with his fingers and let them linger on the tender skin.

Polly sat transfixed, trapped in her chair, while his fingers gently started to stroke her delicate brows. She felt a kind of prickling under her skin which was both delightful and scary. She couldn't have moved even if she had wanted to. And she didn't want to! His caress, as light as the flutter of a bee's wing, was filling her with a delicious kind of languor, and it took every ounce of will power not to sigh, lean back voluptuously, and wait for him to kiss her.

Flint stopped stroking her brows and cupped her face in his hands. 'You've got the sweetest face,' he murmured, 'the sweetest face in the world.'

With a gigantic effort of discipline she jerked her head away and croaked, 'I think I'd better go and cook the fish!'

Thoughtfully he ran his finger down her cheek again, before pulling himself upright and saying, 'Yes—yes, I guess you'd better.' He returned to the drinks tray and added ice to his Cinzano. Polly jammed her feet back into her sandals and hurried to the kitchen.

Dinner was not a great success. She overcooked the salmon and it was dry and chewy, but it didn't seem to matter since neither of them had any appetite. Nor was there any conversation during the meal.

Right after it, Flint excused himself to go and work in the darkroom, and Polly told him that she intended to have an early night. By now she had worked herself into a silent temper and was very off-hand. Hadn't Marjorie always told her that men were faithless—untrustworthy? And didn't Flint's behaviour prove the truth of this opinion? No sooner had Sable's car turned out of the driveway than he had started paying attention to Polly on the pretext of fixing her make-up. He had as good as made a pass, Polly said to herself, resolutely smothering the memory of her quivering response.

When she got up to her room she considered locking her door, but this seemed excessive, even in her mood of self-induced moral indignation. Instead she sat down at the pretty walnut desk and wrote a long letter to her grandmother. She described Crabtree Farm and her new job, and the antics of Duvet and Fellini—but she did not once mention Flint. As if by ignoring him in her letter she could ignore his presence in her thoughts.

CHAPTER SIX

It was with some trepidation that Polly went down to breakfast the next morning, but she need not have worried. Flint was cool and businesslike. Friendly but distant, a far cry from last night. He was also dressed to kill. This was a Flint she had not seen before, a sleek, urban Flint in a raw silk suit and pale shirt, with a silk tie in muted shades of caramel and grey, and hand-made shoes of soft leather. Even his bright thatch of hair lay seal-smooth on his head, as if tamed by his expensive clothes.

He looked so smart that for a moment she regretted her decision to wear her old wrap-skirt again, but her new batik dress seemed a trifle overdone for a day's shopping in Toronto. At least her hair looked great. It had fallen back into shape after her shower as perfectly as when she had left the salon.

Before they went he told her that Sable had phoned late last night to say that the dinner had gone well, and that she was to have an audition this morning, so she had spent the night in her own apartment in town. 'So we'll leave Duvet at Mabel's place,' Flint said, 'it'll be too hot to drag her around with us.'

Polly had wanted to know if it was still all right to go shopping. 'I mean, we could always go another day,' she had said. But he had abruptly told her not to dither, and the subject was dropped.

They went shopping in Toronto's Yorkville area. Originally a village, it had been discovered in the sixties by the hippies, and their coffee houses had taken over and flourished. They had long since left, and it was now an elegant tangle of mews, courtyards and passageways, noted for its chic boutiques and restaurants.

Their first stop was at a tall narrow house, the sand-blasted brick a soft pink, the front door painted brilliant yellow. A brass plate read 'Serendipity', and an outrageous-looking evening dress in peacock hues of striped silk was shown in the tall diamond-paned window.

They entered a spacious room with racks of clothes on each wall, and a glass desk at one end at which sat an exquisitely dressed older woman whose silver-grey hair was piled high on her head in a complicated coiffure. She greeted Flint effusively, sprinkling endearments like confetti at a wedding.

'Darling Flint! Sable told me you were back. How simply *marvellous* to see you.' She kissed his cheek, and at the same time cast an appraising look at Polly.

Flint introduced this resplendent creature, whose name seemed to be Jade, and explained that they wanted to buy several items of clothing.

'Soft colours and soft materials, I think,' he said.

'Polly's the romantic type. And I'm relying on you to give her a good deal, Jade—as a favour to me.'

'Of course, darling,' she cooed, and, turning to Polly, she gave her the kind of scrutiny a farmer might give a young heifer. She nodded her handsome head. 'Mmm! Sloping shoulders, full bust and hips, *and* short . . .'

Thanks a lot! thought Polly, but Jade said brightly,

'I think I've several things that will suit, let's begin, shall we? Change behind that screen,' she waved towards a beautifully embroidered silk screen. 'Then we'll get an idea what's best for you.'

It took two hours. Which amazed Polly, whose idea of buying clothes was to grab a garment in the right size, try it on, and if it fitted reasonably well, pay for it and leave. This was not the system at Serendipity. Polly tried on dozens of dresses. Each time she tried one on she would show herself; Jade would tweak and fuss, and Flint would study her intently and either reject the garment, or suggest a slight alteration which seemed totally unnecessary to Polly, but made an enormous difference once it had been pinned.

Finally her new clothes were chosen. A peach-coloured skirt and matching top, a dress of bleached silk embroidered round the neck with sea-shells, and a cotton dress the colour of ash, sprigged with tiny pink roses. Flint had also insisted she buy a pair of pants in natural cotton, several wide-sleeved tops of different shades, and a faded mauve silk shawl swirled in patterns of purple and green.

'For the evenings,' he told her. 'It's just your style and it'll go with everything.'

They arranged to pick up all these purchases later, to allow time for the alterations. But one dress Polly tried on had fitted perfectly, and this she wore for the remainder of the day. The moment she had slipped it over her head she had fallen in love with it. It was made of cotton challis, which whispered round her hips and fell in a wide bell-like skirt. But it was the colour that enchanted her. It was creamy primrose yellow the bodice was laced over a blush-pink camisole by narrow pink ribbons, and a wider ribbon encircled the waist The inside of the loose short sleeves were lined in blush-pink also, to match the silk petticoat which made a delicate rustling noise when she moved It was a perfect dress! The yellow and pink gave her skin a glow of pale radiance, like a tea rose which still held dew on its petals

When she had stepped from behind the screen to show herself, Jade had said, 'Oh, *yes*!'

But Flint had remained silent, staring at her intently He said only 'Now we must get you proper shoes.' But his voice was not quite steady

On their way to the shoe shop they passed an open-air market. There were stalls with pottery, hand-made jewellery, and other arts and crafts. Hand-braided rugs — like the one in the hall at Crabtree Farm— were hung over a line. Hand-carved furniture, and tables heaped with second-hand clothes and bric-à-brac, filled the sunny yard.

Flint took her arm. 'Let's browse for a bit', he suggested, and she agreed.

It seemed that everyone in the market knew Flint. Polly was introduced to so many people in such a short space of time that her head swam. People came from behind stalls to shake his hand and to tell him that they had missed him. Glamorous young women, and equally glamorous young men, kept coming up to talk, and always when Flint introduced Polly the men gave her hard admiring glances, and she could see them trying to figure out what the relationship was between Flint and herself.

Flint remained suave and totally non-committal. He held Polly's arm in a proprietorial way all the time, and kept them moving steadily through the throng.

They reached a stall piled with small articles of clothing and *objets d'art*. 'I often find props for my work here,' he told her, picking over a bundle of peacock feathers. He held up a yellowed ivory back-scratcher. 'You never know when something like this might come in useful—but not today,' he said to the girl behind the stall. Then he spied something hanging from one of the supports. He reached up and pulled down a large-brimmed straw hat. It had a small bunch of sweet-peas pinned on one side. 'Try this,' he said, putting it on Polly's head and tying the ribbon under her chin. His fingers lingered for a moment and she trembled as he traced the outline of her jaw.

He stepped back and looked at her critically. 'Perfect,' he said softly. He grinned. 'It's perfect, modom,' he kidded her, 'just Modom's style.'

'Oh, I don't know!' Polly said, still flustered by his touch. 'I hadn't budgeted for a hat.'

'My present. No arguments,' Flint held up his strong hand. 'I want to take a picture of you in it, so it can count as a prop.'

He paid the smiling stall owner, and, taking Polly's arm again, he led her away from the market.

After they had bought three pairs of shoes he enquired if she had a swimsuit.

'I have a tank suit.' Marjorie had bought it for her and she had always hated it.

'What colour?'

'A sort of . . . maroon.'

'Not a good colour for you. And a tank suit won't do anything for your type of figure. We've just time before lunch to go to Suits A Person.' He quickened his stride.

'Oh, I don't think I can afford to go there!' she exclaimed, for she knew of the exclusive swimsuit store. She also knew its reputation for high prices.

'I know the two girls who run it—they'll give you a good price. And I can always give you an advance.' She started to demur, but he went on, 'You'll need a decent swimsuit for the picnic. Come on now, Pollyanna! You mustn't spoil the ship for a ha'p'orth of tar!'

By now they had reached the steep stone steps that led

up to the imposing façade of Suits A Person. In the window a black mesh figure modelled a brief silver lamé bikini, and a silver net cover-up was artistically draped to one side of the display. There was no price tag visible, always a sobering sign to Polly. But, undaunted, Flint opened the door and pushed her in ahead of him. The little heels of her new shoes sank into the deep thick carpet, and Polly's heart dropped. It would take her *months* of work to pay Flint back for the advance she was sure she would require to buy a swimsuit from a place like this.

With much foreboding she shook hands with one of the owners and listened while Flint explained what they wanted. He had once done a photo layout in a magazine for this store, so he knew his way around and went unhesitatingly to a rack marked 'Petites', where he started clicking through the hangers, discarding one after the other. Finally he exclaimed,

'Ah! I think we've found it!' and handed it to Polly. 'Try this on, Pollyanna,' he said, 'and then come out and model it.'

In the dressing-room she examined his choice. It seemed to consist of two small pieces of shimmering bronze material held together at the sides by three straps. The legs were cut high, and the front and the back were cut low. She felt very dubious about the whole enterprise.

But when she had it on and looked at herself in the mirror she caught her breath with delight. It fitted like a second iridescent skin, accentuating her compact lushness. At first she looked almost demure, until you caught sight of her naked sides, banded only in the three strips that kept the front of the suit fastened to the back, then she looked sexy and wicked, and as piquant as any model in a fashion magazine. She wouldn't have believed she could ever look like this—and it felt wonderful!

Flint called, 'How are you doing, Pollyanna?' and, taking a deep breath, she opened the door of the dressing-room and stepped out.

He seemed to caress her with his eyes, taking in every curve of her round young body. Her pearl-white skin flushed a delicate pink as his gaze travelled slowly over her full breasts and down to her lush hips. To cover her confusion she pirouetted slowly in an unconscious sensual movement. He didn't say a word.

'It's nice, isn't it?' she volunteered. 'I think I should get it, don't you?'

He cleared his throat before answering. 'Nice? My dear girl, it's *sensational*! I'm not at all sure you should buy it. You might cause a riot.'

'Oh, dear!' She looked down at her bronze-clad front.

'Of course you must get it, Pollyanna,' he laughed. 'But you'd better arrange for police protection whenever you wear it. Now hurry up and change and let's have lunch. I'm starving!' His manner was jocular, but the hand that smoothed back his hair shook slightly.

She paid for the bronze suit, and was pleased to discover that it cost far less than she had anticipated. Not only did she not require an advance, she had a little money left over for a modest assortment of cosmetics.

'But no lipsticks,' Flint commanded. 'You have the mouth of a dreaming child, it would look ludicrous painted.'

Polly, who had secretly planned to indulge in a nice bright lipstick, was momentarily put out by this, but she settled for an untinted lip-gloss without a word of protest.

'Lunch at last!' he said, piloting her towards Bloor Street.

'Where shall we go?' She was still feeling too excited to have much interest in food.

'It's all arranged,' said Flint, 'I've booked us a table at Au Delice.'

She gave a little shriek. 'Oh, Flint! How extravagant,' but she was thrilled, for this was one of the most famous restaurants in Toronto.

'You said you wanted glamour,' he remined her drily. 'I thought I'd better provide it.'

'I've read about Au Delice,' she bubbled, 'it's where all the famous people go to eat——'

Even in her new yellow dress, with her hair falling in fashionable waves about her shoulders, she experienced a moment of insecurity when they entered the magnificent dining-room. It was brightly lit, for, as Flint had said, people came here to be seen. The murmur of the well-modulated voices of the diners mingled with the discreet sound of a trio playing classical music. She longed for a corner to hide in, the way she had hidden at Dexter's party, for she felt out of place in so much muted luxury.

But any insecurity she had soon vanished, for the moment the maître d' spied Flint they were greeted like V.I.P.s. Rather to her surprise, Flint was well known here, too. As they went to their table—a prize one, with a good view of the opulent room—people turned to say hello. Polly recognised an eminent M.P., and a famous T.V. commentator, both of whom greeted Flint by name. A very beautiful actress, renowned for her numerous love-affairs, murmured, 'Flint, darling! I've missed you,' in a husky voice, and shot Polly a venomous look.

Flint smiled enigmatically through all this, nodding to various acquaintances, and all the time holding Polly's arm firmly and possessively, as if she were important to him.

The waiter brought menus and the wine list and asked if Flint would care for his usual aperitif.

'I usually have a brandy sour when I eat here,' Flint told her, 'but I think today we'll have something special.'

He went into a huddle with the wine steward while she looked about her. At one side of the room a fountain played softly. There were huge urns spilling with flowers, and trees in tubs. Light from an enormous skylight played on their leaves. The air smelt faintly of roses and good food, and the tinkling of glassware mingled with the occasional bursts of laughter from the elegant diners.

Flint said, 'I'm going to order your lunch for you, Polly.

There are several dishes on the menu that I think you should sample,' and she was too dazed to do more than fleetingly resent this high-handed treatment.

They didn't talk while they waited for their meal, mainly because people kept coming up to their table to chat to Flint. She was still finding it hard to come to terms with this image of Flint McGregor—man about town. Then it began to dawn on her that all the men who stopped by to talk wanted to meet her too, and the looks they gave her were extremely appreciative.

Whenever one or the other of these males showed signs of becoming extra friendly, Flint would subtly dismiss him, and once, when a particularly persistent man still lingered at their table, his eyes fixed admiringly on Polly, Flint reached for her hand in a proprietorial way. Remembering the tension between them the previous evening, she avoided his grasp.

The waiter arrived with a wine cooler and tall graceful glasses called flutes. He eased the cork from the neck of the bottle and it gave a loud pop.

'Champagne!' exclaimed Polly. 'Oh, Flint, how festive!'

He smiled at her, and she thought what a nice mouth he had, very firm, yet somehow gentle. 'One should always drink champagne at celebrations,' he said.

'Celebrations?'

'Aren't we celebrating the emergence of the new Polly Slater?'

She looked away and took a large swallow of champagne, and a lot of bubbles went up her nose, making her eyes water.

'You're supposed to sip it.' His look was still tender, but now he was laughing, and she felt safer with him.

She smiled back. 'I've never had champagne,' she admitted.

'Well, now that you're launched on this life of glamour I daresay you'll have quite a lot of it,' he teased.

'I won't object.' She took another sip and smiled across

the table at him, but the laughter on his face had died and
he said with great seriousness,

'Don't ever get blasé, Pollyanna. Change the outside
all you want, but don't change the inside. Please. Don't
ever forget that glamorous women are a dime a dozen,
but ladies like Polly Slater are a very rare breed.'

She played with her glass, suddenly wary of him.
'Ladies are a dying breed, I understand,' she said lightly.
'Women are the in thing these days.'

He reached over and stilled her nervous fingers, and
she felt his light touch like a flame through her entire
body. 'Lady is synonymous with woman in my vocabu-
lary,' he said softly, 'and you, Pollyanna, are a "female-
type-woman" to the very tips of your toes. Don't change
that. Don't get brittle for the sake of being smart. The
price would be too high.'

She found his intensity both disturbing and exciting,
and it was the latter emotion that forced her to draw her
hand away and say with false lightness. 'It's a good thing
my mother can't hear you. She has a very different
opinion of "ladies", I can tell you!'

'I wasn't talking to your mother,' he said, and she had
the feeling she had hurt him.

But by the time their lunch arrived he seemed to
recover his spirits and was the old teasing Flint she
recognised. The food was scrumptious, and Polly tasted
things she had never had before, starting with fried
Camembert cheese—golden triangles that melted in her
mouth, served on a bed of deep-fried parsley which was
as crisp and green as lettuce; and finishing with pears
poached in white wine, stuffed with crushed macaroons,
and coated in bitter chocolate.

Over coffee she thanked him for the most superb lunch
she had ever eaten. 'I only hope you don't expect me to
prepare meals like that at Crabtree Farm,' she smiled,
'I'm not quite up to that standard.'

'You could be if you studied,' he said. 'Have you
thought any more about cooking school?'

Before she could reply, a male figure came into the dining-room, caught sight of Flint, and made a bee-line for their table.

'Hey, man!' said Dexter, 'you're in town! Why didn't you let me know? We could have had lunch together.'

'I had a date for lunch with Polly,' Flint said, smiling across the table at her.

'Polly?' Dexter looked across at her too. 'My God— *Polly!* Sweetie ... I didn't recognise you!' He took the chair between them. 'Have you already eaten?'

Flint said laconically, 'Do sit down!' and Polly giggled, but Dexter was oblivious to any sarcasm.

'That's too bad,' he went on. 'If I'd known you were coming to Au Delice I would have joined you.'

'You *have* joined us,' said Flint, and signalled to the waiter for the bill.

Dexter laughed, and, catching the waiter's arm as he was about to leave, ordered a vodka and tonic, then he turned his attention again to Polly. 'You look great, sweetie,' he said, 'just great. Have you finished working for this character here?' He jerked his blond head in Flint's general direction. 'Is that what this lunch is all about?'

Flint answered for her. 'No, she hasn't. She's going to be working with me when I try to make something palatable out of your life for the photo-story.'

Dexter said, 'That's the best news I've had today.' His drink arrived and he raised it in a toast to Polly before taking a swallow. 'That means we'll get to see a lot of each other, sweetie.' He flashed one of his devastating smiles at her.

Polly blushed and stammered something inane about looking forward to it as well, for Dexter's sudden attention was making her feel giddy.

With a distinct edge to his voice, Flint said, 'How's your redheaded friend these days?'

Dexter looked at him. 'Redheaded friend?' he repeated.

'The lady you've been squiring around lately,' Flint reminded him, 'the one you had to rush back to town for the other day.'

An expression of distaste crossed the actor's handsome face. '*That* little affair is dying a very fast death.' He turned back to Polly and dropped his voice a decibel. 'In fact, I think I can safely say that during the last five minutes it's been *buried*.'

All she could think of to say was, 'Oh, dear!' which wasn't very brilliant, but she was overcome, both by Dexter's manifest regard, and by the uneasy feeling that it was irritating Flint. In an attempt to change the subject she asked Dexter how the film was progressing. This turned out to be a clever move, and for the next five minutes Dexter regaled them with anecdotes about the problems he was experiencing both on and off camera.

At the end of a particularly funny story concerning his difficulties with his leading lady, he pulled his chair closer to Polly's and said with fervour, 'Gee, it's great to be with somebody who *listens*. To find a chick who doesn't want to talk all the time.'

'I shouldn't think they get much chance around you,' Flint murmured, but Dexter ignored him.

With the solemnity of one conferring a great favour, he said to Polly, 'Would you like to come on to the set—see me work?'

'Oh, ... *please*!' she replied, turning pale with pleasure.

He lowered his voice to a seductive purr. 'Tell you what, sweetie, come tomorrow. I'll be shooting a love scene. I'd like to get your reaction.' He gave her what could only be described as a leer. 'Maybe you could give me some pointers.'

'She can't come tomorrow,' Flint said firmly. 'She has to work.'

This was news to Polly. 'Work?' she questioned. She thought they had arranged for her to have a few days off, now that the article was finished.

'I have to take some aerial photographs. I need you along,' he told her.

'*Aerial* photographs?' she quailed.

'Yeah! I can't manage the plane and the camera *and* keep notes as well.'

She was going to point out that he had managed it in the past, but something in his expression prevented her. She was beginning to recognise that when his eyes turned that particular icy shade of blue, one had better watch one's step, so she merely smiled across at Dexter and said sweetly, 'It looks as if I'm tied up. Sorry about that.'

'There'll be other times. I'll be in touch,' the actor promised her, his voice soft and thrilling, the way it sounded when he was playing a romantic scene on camera.

Pocketing his credit card, Flint rose to his feet. 'It's time to leave, Polly. You have some dresses to collect, and we can't spend the whole afternoon sitting around in restaurants. Besides, Dex will have to be getting back to work. Otherwise they might shoot a scene without him.'

Dexter laughed at the very idea. 'No way, man! But I guess I should be splitting soon.' His eyes never left Polly. 'It's been great seeing you, sweetie. Just great.' He finally seemed aware of Flint looming over him. 'You too, man. See you around.'

'Sure!' Flint started to leave with Polly in tow. Dexter called after them,

'You'll be at the picnic?'

'It's an assignment,' Flint pointed out dourly, 'I'll be there.'

'I'll be seeing you before then, Polly,' Dexter called.

She nodded but was too overcome to reply. She simply couldn't believe it! Even in her wildest daydreams she had never imagined her favourite actor singling her out for such relentless attention. She was on cloud nine!

Flint, however, didn't share her mood. He was tight-lipped while they collected her parcels, and remained that way for most of the journey back to Caledon, only breaking his silence to answer when she voiced some misgivings about the projected plane ride.

'You need not worry,' he said, 'it's not in the least like climbing trees. In any case,' he added curtly, 'it's high time you crossed that Rubicon.' So she retreated into a daydream, and didn't try to make him chat.

She couldn't think what was the matter with him. She sensed that he was not in a temper, for she had enough knowledge of his tempers now to know that they were sudden and vocal. Not like this aloofness. But sulking was not Flint's way either. He seemed more worried than anything else. Two vertical lines had appeared between his brows, and his usual teasing manner had been replaced by a brooding preoccupation.

Sable was already waiting for them at Crabtree Farm, bubbling over with the possibility of working on the cosmetics account and going to Paris. She had had her hair trimmed while she had been in Toronto and it lay bevelled into severe layers on her neck.

Polly thought that it must be the idea of Sable's career taking off in such a spectacular manner that was causing Flint anxiety. But it was Polly, not Sable, that he kept stealing glances at all evening.

Before she went to bed she thanked him again for a lovely day, and impulsively reached up and kissed him. It seemed to her that he almost flinched when her lips grazed his lean cheek.

After she had disappeared upstairs he remained, standing like a pillar of stone, his eyes more troubled than ever.

CHAPTER SEVEN

BEFORE they left next day for the Toronto Island Airport, Flint spent some time taking photographs of Polly in her new hat, Duvet lent her enthusiastic support and managed to get herself included in a number of shots, knock Polly's hat askew, and generally have a good time.

'Aren't you taking rather a lot of pictures?' Polly asked when he had posed her against yet another background. But, 'Got to justify the purchase of that hat,' was all Flint would say. She calculated that he used a whole roll of film before he called a halt.

After lunch, which they ate with Sable, Polly went upstairs to get ready for their plane ride. She pulled on her old jeans and found that when they were teamed up with one of her new wide-sleeved tops, a pale blue one, and her new cream canvas espadrilles instead of her shabby old sandals, she looked quite presentable. She tied her hair back with a blue ribbon and applied some lip-gloss before going downstairs to join Flint.

When she reached the kitchen she remembered that she would need sun-glasses and she stopped to fish around for them in her straw tote-bag. Flint and Sable were standing talking together on the outside porch, their backs to the room. They apparently didn't hear her enter, for they went on talking without even glancing round.

'. . . and if that's the case there's no reason why I shouldn't go back to my own apartment,' Polly heard Sable say.

'Not *now*,' Flint pleaded. 'Go in to town as much as you want—but I need you here more than ever.' He sounded quite agitated, and Sable gave a low chuckle before saying,

'I'd no idea you were so old-fashioned, Flint.' He gave a muffled reply and she continued, 'Well, okay, if it means that much to you, I'll stay.'

Polly heard him mutter, 'Bless you, Sable,' and, feeling she had intruded too long on a private conversation, she cleared her throat loudly to let them know they could be overheard.

Joining them on the porch she noticed that Sable's

brightly painted lips were curved in amusement, but
Flint looked far from cheerful, and Polly had to admit
she didn't blame him. Sable certainly hadn't seemed very
romantic in her response to his heartfelt plea to remain at
Crabtree Farm. No wonder he was in such a subdued
frame of mind. For although he wasn't as gloomy as he
had been last night, he was still a long way from the
happy-go-lucky Flint of old.

Not that Polly was feeling any too chipper herself. The
prospect of a ride in Flint's plane didn't exactly thrill her,
and when she saw it standing on the runway she didn't
feel much better: it was very pretty, glittering silver and
turquoise in the sunshine, but it looked so fragile! It
didn't seem possible it could get up off the ground, and it
was with grave misgivings that she clambered aboard.

The engine started with a roar, and the little craft
taxied to the end of the runway to await permission for
take-off. Flint, wearing earphones in order to listen in on
the radio traffic, gave her a brief smile and nodded
encouragingly.

When permission came the little plane gave a shudder
and hurled itself down the asphalt. Polly was sure they
were going to drive straight into the water, but before
they reached the end of the runway the ground
miraculously dropped away and they were airborne.

They circled over Hanlan's Point, and some people
sunning themselves on the beach below shaded their eyes
to look at the plane above them. A group of children
stopped digging in the sand and waved. But Polly was
still holding on to the sides of her seat, her knuckles
white, and did not return their greeting. Cautiously she
looked down. The tops of the trees looked like soft green
bundles of cloth.

Flint circled away from the lake towards the city itself,
and they started to gain altitude.

'Where are we going?' Polly shouted over the roar as
they passed the tall needle of Toronto's C.N. Tower.

'Manitoulin Island!' he cried back. 'Rainbow Country.'

A tremor of excitement ran through her and she began to feel less nervous. She had always been fascinated by the idea of Northern Ontario, and the area called Rainbow Country particularly attracted her, for it was known to be spectacularly beautiful and rich with legend. The land of the North American Indian. Land of forests, rainbow-spangled waterfalls, and lakes that take their names from the old Ojibway tongue. And Manitoulin, the world's largest freshwater island, with its thousand miles of coastline and peaceful little towns and villages, bounded on one side by Georgian Bay, and on the other by the twenty-three thousand square miles of mighty Lake Huron.

She relaxed her grip of the sides of her seat and peered down at the city. The skyscrapers looked like a set of children's building blocks from the air, and she felt she could stretch out her hand and pick up one of the tiny cars bustling along the busy highways, they looked so small. Flint had been right—this was nothing like climbing trees. This was *fun*! And by the time they were flying over Caledon, and he had dipped lower to give her an aerial view of the farm, she was thoroughly enjoying herself.

Now the little towns grew sparser and the green of the forests more dense. Ahead of them Georgian Bay shone like crumpled silver foil. When they reached it, Flint headed west.,

'Want to get some shots of Flowerpot Island, off Tobermory!' he shouted, and she nodded and reached into the back seat for her clipboard and his camera.

Over the remarkable water-worn rock chimneys, which resembled giant flowerpots and gave this island its name, he stabilised the plane and, opening his side window, took photos for a minute before returning to the controls. The air blowing into the tiny cabin was cool and sweet, and Polly wondered how on earth she could ever have dreaded this experience.

'Oh, look!' She pointed down to the crystal clear water below where a large white ship ploughed its way over the bay, leaving a wake of swirling foam behind it.

'It's the Big Canoe,' Flint shouted, 'the ferry to Manitoulin.'

'It's *beautiful*!' she shouted back happily. Meaning not just the ship, or the flight, but also sharing this with him. She could think of no one else who could have helped her conquer her fear so easily. And there was certainly nobody she would rather have been with.

'Like flying?' he asked her.

'I *love* it!'

He broke into laughter. 'I told you you would. It's a lot safer than riding your bike, let me tell you!'

Smiling, Polly made a face at him and returned her attention to the scene beneath her. They were flying north again now, and she could see the contour of Manitoulin Island in the distance. It seemed that everywhere she looked, her eye was greeted with the glint and hue of water. Closer to Manitoulin itself, she could make out the countless little islands that ringed it, like a flotilla of small craft around a majestic liner.

They flew over the island, and Flint took photographs of Onaping Falls, where the Onaping river drops a hundred and fifty feet in one foaming plunge. And the sandy beaches of Providence Bay, and the lighthouse at treacherous Mississaugi Strait, where the French explorer La Salle's boat *Griffin* was wrecked in 1670.

It was dusk when they turned back for Toronto. It seemed to Polly that the water was choppier than it had been, but it was hard to see in the gathering dark. In any case, she wasn't worried, for the little plane seemed to her now as stable as granite as it buzzed its way over the vast expanse of water below. Then, without an warning at all, the engine faltered and coughed into silence. The only sound now was the whistling of the wind as they started to lose height.

Flint began to flip the switch on the plane's electronic locator transmitter, at the same time radioing the international distress signal—'Mayday'. Polly could hear a loud 'whooping' noise from the earphones he had pulled off.

'Flint! What's happening?' she screamed.

'We're going to ditch in the lake,' he said, reaching in behind her seat where the life raft was stowed. 'Strap in tightly, fold your arms across your forehead and lean forward and rest on the panel. When the plane stops bouncing, open the door and get out fast!'

Horrified, Polly took a quick glance into the darkness before she obeyed his command. It seemed to her that the crested tops of sizeable waves seemed to be rushing towards them at alarming speed.

Before she had time to dwell on this unpleasant phenomenon, the belly of the aircraft hit the lake with a shuddering thump. Water started to swamp the cabin, swirling round their ankles in a rushing flood.

'Quick!' said Flint urgently, 'we're going down.' Swiftly he activated the CO_2 bottle to inflate the raft, and, opening her door, threw it out, pushing her after it. 'Here!' He reached for the survival kit which had been stored next to the raft. 'Hang on to that!' and heaving the life-raft clear of the sinking plane, he dove into the water.

'Flint!' shrieked Polly, for the raft was bobbing up and down on the choppy waves and she couldn't see him. 'Flint! . . . Oh, my God! . . . Flint, where are you?'

'I'm here. Don't panic.' His voice was close, and she now saw that he had swum to her and was clinging to the side of the raft. 'There isn't room for both of us, we'll have to take turns in the water. If you can swim, that is.'

She said, 'Y—yes. I'm a very g—good swimmer,' and then she gulped hard, for she was so happy to know that he was safe she felt quite tearful.

She noticed that the raft was equipped with a pair of collapsible oars clipped to the inside, and she asked if she should row.

'Not much point,' replied Flint, pulling himself into a more secure position. 'We don't know where we're going. Save your energy for when we sight land.'

She peered into the blackness, trying to see the shape of the plane, but it had disappeared. It was hard to see very far since it was a moonless night and the water was quite rough. The raft kept being lifted up on the crests of waves, then sucked down into watery troughs again. Flint had his elbows hooked over the rim of the raft. He was wearing a bright yellow jacket, which made it easier for her to see him, and after a while her eyes began to get used to the dark.

'Where are we?' she asked.

'In Lake Huron.'

'I know *that!*' she said shortly. Now that the shock of the forced landing was past, she was feeling irritable. *'Where* in Lake Huron?'

'I don't know for sure. Near Tobermory is my guess.' He tightened his hold on the life raft as a larger wave buffeted them. 'There are lots of islands around. We should sight one soon. When we do, we'll land and make camp.' He sounded quite matter-of-fact, and this calmed her.

She remembered his pretty little plane sinking without a trace and felt a stab of contrition for her bad temper. Putting her hand on his wet arm, she exclaimed, 'Oh, Flint! Your plane!'

'We're safe, Pollyanna. That's all the matters,' he replied, and she smiled wanly because she wasn't at all sure that they were. 'Now, if you're up to it, maybe you could take a turn in the water. My legs are cold, and my arms could use a rest!'

She took off her espadrilles and slipped into the water, and he pulled himself into the raft. She was already quite wet, for she had been liberally splashed by the waves. And she was cold, for the wind was chill. But it felt as warm as a summer breeze in contrast to the lake. She hung over the side, the way he had done, so her legs and thighs were in the water. Flint tied a guy-rope around her waist so that she couldn't drift away, and he leaned towards her, with his hands lightly on her arms so she wouldn't feel alone.

But in spite of this she still felt like a very small cork on a very large body of water, and by the time she had alternated floating and being in the raft three times she began to feel desperate.

About this time Flint tensed—it was his turn in the raft. He said, 'I think I see something ahead. Hang on! I'm going to row.' He fitted the oars together, inserted them in the rubber oarlocks on either side of the boat, and started rowing hard. Polly kicked her legs in the water to help their progress.

Gradually the shape of a tiny island materialised out of the night.

'Land!' Flint cried triumphantly. 'Land, Pollyanna. We'll be drinking hot coffee before you know it!'

And then what? she thought, shivering, but she kicked at the water harder than ever, and soon they were only a few yards from the steep granite cliffs of the island.

'How are we going to get up *there?*' she queried breathlessly, but Flint merely said,

'It'll be okay,' and started to row round to the other side.

He was right. Here several smooth boulders lay, like a shallow staircase, making it easy to clamber up on to dry land. He gave a last pull at the oars and the raft grounded with a faint hiss on the wet stone.

Polly's knees grazed the surface of the rock, and she tried to stand, but forgot she was still fastened to the raft by the guy-rope and, losing her balance, she fell to her knees again. In seconds Flint was beside her; he undid the knot, and, putting his powerful arms round her waist he half dragged, half carried her ashore, where she lay on her stomach, panting like a beached fish. After he had pulled their raft out of the water he collapsed beside her.

She took a shuddering breath and turned on her side to

look at him. 'Flint McGregor,' she gasped 'if you ever say another word about my driving I'll kill you!'

Pulling himself into a sitting position, he smile wryly. 'I promise to lay off.' He clambered to his feet. 'Now, let's make camp and dry ourselves out.

She took the hand he offered and let him pull her upright. The wind made her soaking clothes feel like ice on her skin, and she started to tremble from the cold.

'The first thing we must do is build a fire,' he said, putting his arm round her again as she shivered. Although he was no warmer than she, it felt good to have him so close, and instinctively she cuddled closer. 'I'll make us a shelter if you'll search for dry wood. There should be quite a bit of it about inland.'

She looked at the tangle of dark trees ahead of them, a black mass against the cloudy sky. 'How will I find my way?'

'With a great deal of difficulty,' he said drily. 'Pick up any wood you stumble over that's not too big to carry. I'll build us a wind-break over by that tree.' He pointed to an outcrop of rock where the roots of a large spruce clung to the meagre soil. Taking off his soaking yellow jacket, he handed it to her. 'Use this as a basket. Now—off you go. And watch our for poison ivy!'

'What a jolly day this is turning out to be,' said Polly as she climbed into the underbrush. 'All I need is to get covered in poison ivy blisters to make it perfect!'

She filled Flint's jacket with dry wood and pine-cones and added several larger branches for good measure—just to show him! By the time she returned to their stony beach he had fixed a pine-bough lean-to and was unpacking various small packets from the survival kit.

'Ah, good!' he said as he took the pile from her. 'I've fixed up a clothes line out of the guy-rope. You undo this,' he handed her a small plastic bag the size of a cigarette packet.

'What is it?' It felt soft and made a sound like tissue paper when she squeezed it.

'It's a Space Blanket An emergency blanket It's made out of garbage-bag material When you've undone it, take your wet things off and wrap yourself in it You'll be warm again in no time flat

'Take my clothes off?'

'Of course, you'll catch your death if you don't You can undress behind the spruce The thing's seven feet long, for God's sake!' he snapped when she hesitated 'You'll be perfectly covered!'

She went behind the spruce and removed the gold foil from its plastic cover. He was right about it being big! It took her about five minutes to unwrap it! It was silver on one side, gold on the other, and as thin as a sheet of plastic kitchen wrap.

She peeled off her jeans, which were now unpleasantly damp rather than wringing wet, pulled off her blue top and rolled it into a ball with her bra and bikini panties. Then, with the gold side next to her skin, she folded the blanket round her naked body.

It was rather difficult walking back to the shelter wrapped in seven feet of foil and she tripped over her trailing hem quite often, but she managed not to fall down.

Flint had laid a fire and was in the act of lighting it. When he saw her—a small, silvery figure, her hair a tangled mass of feathery curls round her face—he remained motionless for a moment. 'You look like a particularly delicious ghost,' he said at last, and struck a match against a stone. The twigs crackled to life, and orange-tongued flames started to lick the branches.

'Aren't we lucky the matches didn't get wet,' she said. She had to struggle to keep her voice from trembling, for she was very conscious that she was stark naked under the flimsy sheet, and she knew that Flint was aware of it too.

'Luck has nothing to do with it,' he replied. 'I filled an empty film can with two kinds of matches and dipped their heads in wax so they'd be protected. And *then* I wrapped the whole thing in wax-soaked cotton batten. Without my foresight, my girl, your undies wouldn't get dry.' He held out his hand and, rather embarrassed, she handed him her bundle of damp clothes which he proceeded to string on the makeshift line.

He stripped off his wet shirt and hung it up too. 'Might as well dry off the top half of me,' he said. The light from the flames illuminated his broad chest which was lightly sprinkled with dark red hair, and made his golden skin look like polished bronze.

He squatted down beside the raft which he had pulled up into the lee of the lean-to where it could be used as a seat. 'Which would you prefer?' he asked, holding aloft two pouches. 'Shrimp Creole or Boeuf Bourguignon?'

She stared at him. 'What do you mean?'

He waved the pouches at her. 'Freeze-dried dinners. Isn't science wonderful? Now you choose, Pollyanna. Which is it to be?'

Under the circumstances this sophisticated fare seemed very inappropriate, and she giggled, 'What kind of wine will you be serving?'

'Eau de Huron!' he gestured to the lake. 'Boiled and flavoured with coffee crystals.'

'In that case, let's have the beef,' she decided.

When he had fixed the pot over the fire she asked nervously, 'How much food do we have? I mean . . . shouldn't we ration ourselves or something?'

'We've got plenty. Besides, we'll be picked up soon, I promise.'

'Oh, I see.' She was not convinced, however.

He came and sat beside her, putting his arm around her shoulders. 'I'm not saying that to make you feel better, sweetheart,' he lied. 'Before we left Toronto I filed our flight plan. When we came down I activated the E.L.T. and transmitted a Mayday. They're probably looking for us at this moment.' He hugged her closer. 'There's nothing to worry about, I promise you.' He omitted to add that he didn't know for certain that his

Mayday message had been picked up.

Her heart was pounding, but not because of the fear of being stranded. Every inch of her was aware of him. Every inch of her wanted him to hold her closer still, and call her sweetheart, and . . .

'Sable will be worried out of her mind,' she said, regaining her sanity and moving subtly away from him.

Flint rose and put more wood on the fire. 'Yeah! Your mother too, I'm afraid. It's sure to have been announced on the news.'

'Oh dear,' said Polly, 'what a nuisance!' She could hear Marjorie now, blaming Flint for the whole accident. In her mother's eyes the simple fact that he was a male would make him responsible for the engine failure, the ditching in the lake, the worry; *everything*. That he had managed to land them safely and unhurt would be dismissed.

'There's nothing we can about it, it's just bad luck.' He smiled ruefully. 'I guess this has put you off flying, eh?'

Polly thought for a minute. She remembered the pleasure she had experienced earlier. The feeling of freedom, of being in a new dimension. Rather to her surprise she discovered that her newly acquired taste for flying had not been extinguished. But she knew this was mainly because she trusted Flint. If he was at the controls she would not experience a moment's fear.

'I'm not put off,' she said, then added, 'but I *am* hungry. How long before dinner?' because she didn't want to say anything that he might think of as a complimentary, and therefore provocative, remark.

The Beouf Bourguignon—which was surprisingly good—and the hot coffee, which wasn't, warmed her thoroughly. The sky cleared, and the moon, looking like a silver bubble, shone on the water. A scattering of stars appeared.

Flint collected more wood and built up a fire. 'The time has come, Pollyanna, to tell you how great you are,' he said. 'I can't think of anyone I'd rather be marooned with.'

She was delighted with his good opinion, but she was also cautious, for she was aware of a growing intimacy between them. We're positively domestic! she thought, with the shared meal and my undies hanging on the line. So, all she said was,

'Better not speak to soon. I might have screaming hysterics tomorrow.'

'There you go! Underestimating yourself again!' He slipped an arm around her shoulder and gave her a brief hug. 'You're a plucky girl; none better. Take it from me.'

'Yes—well. . . .' Flustered, she pulled herself to her feet and stumbled towards the clothes-line. 'I wonder if my clothes are dry yet?'

'You won't need them till the morning,' he said, rising and coming towards her. 'You'll sleep much better in just the space blanket.'

'Oh—yes . . .' Polly clutched the foil sheet tightly over her breasts.

He stood in front of her and gently tilted her chin so that she was looking up into his eyes which were as dark as blue diamonds in the shadowed night.

'Do you have any idea how pretty you are, Pollyanna?' he whispered. 'Like a lovely silver statue in the moonlight.'

He bent his head and kissed her gently on the mouth. At the touch of his lips the stars swung out of their places and back again, leaving her dizzy and breathless.

He drew away, and the surprise on her face was mirrored in his.

Wordlessly he lifted her in his arms and carried her back to the fire, and when they were sitting against the life-raft he kissed her again, but this time his mouth was demanding, searching.

Her own lips parted and her heart turned over with desire. Without thought or caution now, she put her arms round his neck to draw him closer and the slippery edges of the foil slid open exposing one silky breast. A tide of feeling crept up in her, strong and fierce. But it did not frighten her. It filled her with a strange, deep joy, and when Flint's hand found her round breast she pressed closer to him in an ecstasy of passionate abandon.

Tenderly he pulled the foil sheet up over her shoulders so that her breasts were covered. 'You are beautiful, Pollyanna,' he said huskily, 'but I mustn't. It wouldn't be fair.'

A flood of shame swept over her. Of course it wouldn't be fair! She had forgotten Sable. She had forgotten *everything!* She had only been conscious of the taste of his lips and his deft caresses. One kiss in the moonlight and she had behaved like a wayward trollop! His for the taking. It had been up to Flint to remind her—to remind them both—that he was committed to another woman.

So much for Marjorie's theory that men—all men—would take whatever advantage they could. Flint McGregor appeared to be made from different clay.

'There's a little hollow under the tree,' he said, 'it should be fairly comfortable for you to sleep in. I'll make you a pillow of spruce.'

His voice was controlled, but she had no notion of the effort this cost him. She's a *child!* thought Flint. An innocent child quivering on the edge of womanhood. God, it would have been so easy to betray that innocence. But I can't take advantage of that. I must take time to awaken her, so that when she says "yes", she will fully understand herself—and me—and what she's saying "yes" to.

He smiled ironically in the dark as he broke off another frond of spruce. I can't figure myself out, he thought. I'm turning into a regular Sir Galahad. Any other girl and we'd have been *very* cosy by now! But she's different, is Polly . . . as intense as T.N.T.! And special— very, very special.

He finished making the pillow. 'There you are, ma'am,' he said, 'your bed's turned down for the night.'

'Thank you.' She was huddled by the life-raft. A waif in silver.

Offering his hand, he helped her to her feet, then watched her with disturbing steadiness. 'Don't worry about anything, Pollyanna. You need a good night's sleep. You've had quite a day, remember. Things will look different in the morning.'

She nodded. She wanted to ask where *he* was going to sleep, but was afraid it might sound like a sexual come-on, so she merely said, 'Good night, then,' and lay down in the hollow. The spruce smelt delicious under her head.

She was tired to the point of exhaustion, but she didn't sleep right away. Her mind kept skidding back to the moment when Flint had held her in his arms, and she had lost track of time and place, and her own identity.

I must be utterly *depraved* to have behaved like that with *Flint,* she thought miserably. After all, it's Dexter I'm mad about. Flint's just my boss. And if I react that way when Flint kisses me, how will I react if *Dexter* ever makes love to me? And she felt the soft cheek that was pillowed on her hand burn scarlet in the darkness.

She heard Flint moving quietly to a place at the other end of the lean-to, and, turning on her side, saw him lay his long body down on the rock. He had put his shirt on again, and was using his yellow jacket as a pillow. He looked extremely uncomfortable.

Hastily she suppressed the thought that it would be nice to be curled beside him, cradled together on her bed of spruce.

When sleep finally claimed her she slept heavily and without dreaming and came to at dawn. The sun was rising and the sky was smudged with delicate bands of soft, creamy pink. She looked at the place where Flint had been sleeping. It was empty. Then she noticed that a piece of paper, torn from the log book, was by her head. It was anchored by a small bar of soap. Sitting up, she read Flint's note.

"Good morning, Sleeping Beauty. I've gone off to

explore the terrain. Just had a bath in the lake and I've left you the soap. The water's great! I'll give a whistle when I come back and wait five minutes to give you time to dress. F.'

She climbed stiffly to her feet. Her bones ached from the hard ground, and her skin felt gritty. The unruffled surface of the lake was shrouded with floating veils of silver mist. It beckoned enticingly. But she wouldn't risk staying too long in the still, dark water. She didn't want Flint to find her stark naked, splashing about in the shallows. He might think she had delayed getting dressed in order to titillate him, so, grabbing the soap, she hurried to the water's edge, unwrapping her blanket as she went.

She spent the minimum amount of time in the water—which was a shame, for it was cool and delicious, coloured a dark amber and soft as silk. But she was driven by the desire to eradicate any image he might have of her as a seductress, so she pulled on her clothes over her wet body. One of her knees poked through a ragged hole in her jeans, and her ribbon was missing.

She was gathering more driftwood for their fire by the time Flint's piercing whistle floated into the still morning. When he finally joined her, she was shocked at how tired he looked, his usually brilliant eyes dull, and the skin beneath them smudged with fatigue. The lines of his face seemd to have been etched deeper.

The maternal instinct in her got the better of her enforced reserve, and she put her hand on his bare arm. 'I'll make the coffee,' she said firmly, 'you sit down and try to relax. Is there anything to eat?'

'Bossy, bossy!' he muttered, but he did as she said without any argument. 'There's the shrimp, but I don't think I can face that for breakfast. Apart from that, there's plenty of glop.'

'Glop?' Her hazel eyes widened. 'What on earth's that? It sounds revolting!'

He smiled his lopsided smile. 'It's a mixture of rolled

oats, raisins and nuts. Delicious!'

'Then glop it is,' she said, 'and hot coffee. Now you sit still. You look done-in.'

He lay back on the rocks, which were already getting warm from the sun, and watched her as she bustled about, filling the pan with water, measuring coffee into the collapsible plastic mugs.

'What a motherly little soul you are,' he remarked when he handed him his share of the oatmeal mixture, insisting that he have most of the raisins because they were good for energy.

Since Polly had heard her mother say the same thing as a criticism she bridled, and said gruffly, 'It's the way I was born. I can't help it.'

He looked at her wearily. 'No need to get defensive. I meant it as a compliment. Being motherly is a special kind of caring, I think, and it takes a special kind of talent.'

'Does it?' Thoughtfully Polly chewed on a peanut. 'I never thought of it like that.'

'Well, start!' His voice was rough with fatigue. 'I realise I'm knocking my head against a brick wall. You've been brainwashed. But, for the record, it's my opinion that the woman who is endowed with the gift of creating and running a home has the greatest talent of all. A talent for loving. And I think you have that, Polly. Just look what you've done to the farm.'

'I've only cooked a few meals,' she said.

'And served them with style. And seen that there are fresh wild flowers on the table, and an arrangement of dried grasses in front of the fireplace in the kitchen . . .

'Oh, that!'

'Yes, *that!* And the silver bowl in the dining-room shining and filled with fresh fruit, and nice little soaps in the bathrooms and all that stuff. Mabel didn't do it. She's good at keeping the place clean, but she doesn't know anything about the little touches that make a house a home. You do.'

She licked her fingers. 'I didn't think you'd noticed; you never said anything.'

'I noticed. And appreciated it. But I knew you'd do your usual trick of dismissing it as "nothing" if I mentioned it, so what was the use?'

'I'm going to stop doing that,' she told him. 'It's a bad habit and I intend to break it.'

'About time!' Flint stroked the dark coppery growth on his face. 'My chin feels like a cheese grater,' he said, yawning prodigiously. 'I think I'll lie down and grab forty winks under your tree. I'm bushed. Would you spread my jacket out on the beach? It'll make it easier for them to spot us.'

He fell asleep almost at once, and when she had found a prominent spot for the yellow jacket, and washed and re-packed their mugs, she sat on a rock and paddled her feet in the lake. She had meant what she had said about disciplining herself not to constantly sell herself short. The past couple of weeks had taught her that she had value. She, Polly Slater, the girl with no talent, had coped with a new job and different surroundings without turning a hair. She had conquered her shyness and made new friends, and she felt useful and needed.

If only she could erase the memory of her scandalous behaviour with Flint last night she would feel completely at ease with herself. It was all very well to have . . . what had he called it? A talent for loving. That didn't mean she had to abandon herself every time a man kissed her! She still burned at the thought, but no matter how hard she fought it the recollection of his lips on hers still gave her a thrill of pleasure.

It was about this time she heard the sound of a plane. Flint woke in a second and came running down to the water's edge, picking up his jacket and waving it about his head to attract attention. But this activity was unnecessary. They had been spotted.

The plane circled low and dropped a canister with a

red streamer attached to it. It fell into the bush behind them.

'What are they doing?' Polly asked.

'They're trying to establish our identity. Come on!' he grabbed her hand. 'Come and help me find it.'

It was only a matter of minutes before they had spotted the streamer caught in a bush and Flint had pulled the canister free. Inside were matches, food, a first-aid kit, flares, and a note which read, 'If you are Angus McGregor and passenger, fire a red flare.'

'What are they sending letters for?' wailed Polly indignantly, 'Why don't they rescue us and be done with it?'

'They're just being tactful,' he explained as they hurried back to the beach. 'We might not *want* to be rescued!' There was a wicked gleam in his eyes as he readied the flare. 'What do you say, Pollyanna?' he teased, holding up a match. 'Shall I send the flare—or not?'

But Polly refused to enter into this erotic game. 'Don't be *ridiculous,*' she snapped. 'Send off the damn flare before they lose interest and go.'

With a grin he lit it, and they both watched the plane dip its wings in acknowledgement before flying off.

By the time they had cleaned up their camp they heard a rasping buzz and soon the bright yellow rescue helicopter was hovering above them, for the terrain made it impossible for it to land. Two Sea Air Rescue technicians wearing orange coveralls were lowered down on a winch affair that she later learned was called a Sky Genie.

'Welcome to our island,' Flint greeted them genially. 'We've had a great time, but we're really happy to see you guys, aren't we, Pollyanna?'

She nodded weakly. 'How—how do we—get up there?' She indicated the aircraft hovering above.

'No problem, lady,' the techs assured her. 'They'll winch us up, and one of us comes along for the ride, too.'

'Think of it as a swing in a playground,' Flint urged quietly. 'After all you've been through this should be a piece of cake.'

But it wasn't *quite* that easy, and when she had been strapped in to the harness she froze with fear, looking down in dismay at the tilting ground below.

Then she saw Flint standing beneath her, giving her the 'thumbs up' sign, and when the flight engineer helped her into the helicopter no one would have guessed that she had not been riding in Sky Genies all her life. Except Flint—but that was okay because he was her friend, and she could tell by his expression that he was proud of her.

Back on the mainland, they went through the required routine of a medical examination and a report was given to the police and Department of Transport.

The pilot, who knew Flint (it seemed to Polly that *everybody* knew Flint), agreed to fly them all the way back to Toronto, to save them having to arrange for transportation from the mainland.

'A lot of folks will be real glad you guys have been found,' the pilot said, and she gathered that their disappearance had created quite a stir, so she wasn't surprised when they dropped down on to the landing pad to see a group of people waiting for them. What did surprise her was the number of news photographers, and the sight of a television crew. She knew Flint was well known in his field, but she had no idea he rated this kind of attention.

Neither, apparently, did he, for she heard him say, 'What the hell?' under his breath.

'What's all this in aid of?' he asked the pilot.

'You had some pretty famous people worried,' the man grinned. 'They made a lot of noise!'

They climbed down on to the ground and the photographers surged forward, the reporters with them, pens at the ready. Polly caught sight of Marjorie, white-faced and without her usual cigarette. 'Mom!' she called, and hurried towards her. With an unusual display of affection, Marjorie hugged her close. Then she broke loose.

'What the hell happened?' she snorted to cover her emotion.

'Engine failure . . . Flint was marvellous,' said Polly, anticipating her mother's criticism.

'Looks like it,' growled Marjorie. 'What did he fly before? Kites?'

Before Polly could jump to his defence the photographers descended, begging them to hug again so they could take pictures.

'Get lost!' snapped Marjorie, taking Polly's hand and dragging her towards the small building that served as a lounge for the helicopter station. 'Take pictures of the movie star. He likes that kind of thing.'

'Movie star!' exclaimed Polly. She began to understand why the press was here in full force. 'Is Dexter responsible for all this fuss?' Then she saw him. He stood waiting by a TV camea, Sable just behind him.

'Sweetie!' he called, and she saw him give a nod to the cameraman. He held out his arms. She had the impression that she was expected to run into them, and that was the moment was being filmed for publicity purposes.

'Hi, Dexter,' she replied, stubbornly standing where she was. 'What are you doing her?'

The famous star looked momentarily put out, then he smiled broadly and came up to her, embracing her fondly before turning to the camera.

'Thanks, Mr. Grant,' said the cameraman. 'That'll look great on the six o'clock new.' He left to go to Flint who was still on the landing pad.

Sable came up and kissed Polly on the cheek. 'You had us all worried for a while there, Polly,' she said. 'Welcome back. There's hot coffee in the lounge. I guess we could all use a cup.'

'We can go home as soon as you like,' Marjorie said pointedly to Polly as they went into the building. 'I've got the day off'

'First there's to be a short press conference,' Dexter
told them. 'We want to know about this poor baby's
ordeal first hand.' Sable went to a table at the far side of
the room and started pouring coffee into styrofoam cups

Remembering her manners, Polly began to introduce
Dexter to her mother, but he forestalled her.

'I've already met your mother, sweetie. When I heard
Flint's plane had gone down, and remembered that you
were with him, I called on your mother and introduced
myself.' He smiled brilliantly at Marjorie, who threw him
a look of intense dislike. 'I figured she'd need a bit of
moral support.'

He led the women to a group of chairs. Sable joined
them, carrying a tin tray of coffee which she put down on
the low table, first clearing a space among the clutter of
ash-trays and dog-eared magazines. 'I wasn't too
worried, really,' she said, handing Polly a cup of coffee. 'I
knew you'd be all right with Flint.'

Polly took the cup gratefully. Now that she was safely
on land again she was beginning to feel wobbly. She
smiled up at Sable. 'Flint was wonderful,' she concurred,
'you must be very proud of him.'

Looking rather startled, Sable said, 'Well . . . of course
. . . he's a terrific pilot.'

Polly thought it rather strange that Sable didn't run out
to Flint and throw herself into his arms. If Flint was *my*
lover I'd let him know that I was happy to see him safe
and sound, Polly thought, and wondered, in that case,
why she was finding Dexter's attentions so irritating. All
this 'poor baby's ordeal' rubbish was definitely getting on
her nerves.

Flint came in to the lounge. He looks *so* tired, thought
Polly, this excitement is the last thing he needs. I wonder
why Dexter dreamed up this welcoming committee
anyway? For she was positive the press was there at the
actor's invitation.

After Sable had given Flint a very undemonstrative

hug he went over to where Marjorie was sitting 'I'm very sorry, Ms Slater, for the anxiety I must have caused you,' he said 'Polly wasn't really in any danger, but you weren't to know that '

Marjorie fumbled in her battered denim bag for a cigarette before answering 'I didn't suppose you'd crashed on purpose ' She flicked at her lighter 'In any case, it was your friend here who panicked, not me ' She blew a thin stream of smoke in Dexter's direction.

Dexter looked pained 'Of *course* I panicked,' he remonstrated. 'My best friend, and the cutest little chick I've met in years, missing over that lake— I was worried out of my skull!'

'My daughter was not hatched out of an egg!' Marjorie glared at him.

Polly said hastily, 'I think I want to go home now,' because she didn't think she could take an altercation between Dexter and her mother at that moment.

'Do you have transport?' Flint asked Marjorie, who told him she had her car. 'Then I think it would be a good idea to take Polly home to bed,' he said. 'She must be worn out.' He waited while the older woman stubbed out her cigarette, then he added, 'You would have been very proud if you'd have seen how your daughter coped in a very difficult situation, Ms Slater. She's a very brave girl.'

'I wouldn't expect her to behave badly,' Marjorie said gruffly. But Polly knew she was pleased.

'But the press conference!' wailed Dexter. 'I told them we'd give them a story as soon as you'd had coffee.'

'*I'll* give them their story,' Flint said firmly, 'you don't need Polly for that.'

'Okay, but one picture before you go,' Dexter said to Polly, and without waiting for a reply he went to the door and called in the photographers. 'One shot of me with Miss Slater, guys,' he said, putting his arm round her shoulders. 'The safe return of the girl of my dreams.'

Polly turned bright scarlet. She knew she should have

been delighted by her idol's attention, but she wished it weren't so public. 'Flint should be in the picture, too,' she suggested. 'I mean—I wasn't exactly alone.'

'But *you* were the one I was out of my wits about,' Dexter murmured as the cameras clicked.

'Are you *coming*, Polly?' Marjorie was standing by the door, her face a mask of distaste.

'Yes, Mom.' Thankfully she eased herself out of Dexter's embrace.

He called after her, 'I suddenly realised what I'd been missing in my life. Get prepared for a lot of attention, sweetie!'

'Come *on*, Polly!' Marjorie called impatiently. She nodded curtly to Flint. 'Goodbye, Mr. McGregor.' She ignored the others.

Flint inclined his head. He looked grim. 'I'll be in touch after a few days, Polly,' he said, 'to discuss our working schedule.'

'I'll be in touch *before* that,' Dexter assured her. 'Having found you, I'm never going to let you go again!' He smiled fondly as she went out after her mother.

But the expressions that remained printed on Polly's memory were Flint's worried frown, and Sable's unaccountably stricken face.

CHAPTER EIGHT

THE first three days of Polly's holidays were spent cleaning and tidying the house. No housekeeper at the best of times, Marjorie had excelled herself in creating a mess. Polly worked steadily, almost enjoying the tedium of housework, since it helped to take her mind off her present life, which suddenly seemed complicated.

For nineteen years she had lived a humdrum existence, and dreamed of a life filled with glamour and excitement, and overnight her dreams appeared to have become reality.

She wasn't sure she was enjoying it.

For instance, she should have been thrilled when enormous bunches of flowers started arriving from Dexter. In one day alone she received a sheaf of orchids, two dozen gladioli and a spray of camellias. But the fact was, it was *too much*. Besides, she preferred less exotic blooms.

On the third day, when the grinning florist delivered a huge bunch of gardenias and twelve white lilies, she groaned aloud.

'Where am I going to put them?' she muttered wildly, searching under the stairs for empty jam jars. She had phoned Dexter to thank him and had hinted that she lived in a small house and didn't possess any vases. The second time she had called she had said outright that she had run out of containers, but he had obviously not paid any attention, being far too wrapped up in himself and the pressure of finishing his film.

She was attempting to plug the hole in an old lamp base, thinking this might serve as a vase for the lilies, when her mother arrived home from work.

'Who died?' she asked, surveying the creamy blossoms with a jaundiced eye.

Ignoring this, Polly filled the lamp base with water. Immediately the cork she had tried to jam in the hole fell out and water gushed over the kitchen counter. Swearing, she pushed her wet fingers through her tumbled brown curls.

'Could I borrow your car after supper, Mom?' she asked. 'I think I'll drive over and donate these flowers to the hospital.'

'Good idea,' said her mother, sitting down at the kitchen table and lighting a cigarette. 'I take it these are from that moronic actor, too?'

Polly was at once on the defensive. 'If you mean Dexter the answer is yes. And I think it's very nice of him to send me flowers.'

'*Flowers* is one thing. An entire florist's *shop* is another. Besides, it's a chauvinistic seductive game that I thoroughly disapprove of.' Contemptuously Marjorie picked up a lily that had fallen on the floor. 'I suppose when he turns up in person he'll be carrying a box of chocolates shaped like a heart.'

'Oh, do give it a rest, Mom!' Polly snapped back, stung into a temper by her mother's jeering. 'I don't expect you to approve. You hate Dexter just because he's a *man!*' Her golden eyes glittered with anger. 'You hate *all* men on principle, I know that.'

Marjorie made a smoke ring. She wasn't used to seeing the usually placid Polly in a temper. 'That's not true,' she said, 'I don't hate all men. I quite like Flint McGregor, as a matter of fact.'

'Well, well!' mocked Polly. 'What did Flint do to earn this unexpected praise?'

'He didn't *do* anything. That's the whole point. He strikes me as the type who doesn't play games. I respect that. I wish *he* was the one you liked, rather than this . . . this *actor!*'

'I like Flint,' Polly said. 'He just doesn't have Dexter's . . . charisma. And as for playing games——' It was on the tip of her tongue to tell Marjorie about Flint making love to her on the island, but instead she said, 'I'm sure he could "play games" as you call it, if he fancied me. But he's got a girl.'

Marjorie stubbed out her cigarette. All at once the tough mask she wore had slipped away and she looked much younger, vulnerable. 'Be careful, Poll,' she said earnestly. 'Don't be taken in—the way I was. I couldn't bear for you to be hurt.'

Polly's temper vanished like mist in the sun and she came to sit opposite her mother. Stretching out her hand to take Marjorie's nicotine-stained fingers, she assured her, 'Don't worry, love—I'll be all right. But I can't help enjoying a bit of attention. No matter what you may believe, it's fun.'

'I know it is. That's the trouble!' Marjorie said gloomily, drawing her hand away. 'But frankly, I don't trust this actor further than I can throw him.'

Exasperated again, Polly got up and started wrapping her flowers in a wet paper towel to preserve them. 'For your information, Dexter has always behaved perfectly,' she snapped, 'and I think he's *marvellous*. I'm *crazy* about him. So let's just drop the subject, okay?' She was over-stating her true feelings for Dexter. Actually her attraction to him had been eroded over the past week, and now she found him charming but shallow. She hardly dared admit it to herself, but he was beginning to bore her. The way Flint never could. But by attacking Dexter the way she had, Marjorie had forced Polly to feel protective towards him.

And also Polly felt resentful towards Flint, who had stirred her so incredibly with his kisses, and then rejected her. He hadn't phoned *once* in the three days she had been home, and she was mysteriously hurt by his lack of attention.

Driving home from the hospital later that evening she decided she would regain the passion she had felt for Dexter in the past. She would consciously work on it! That way she would relegate Flint McGregor back to where he belonged, to a subordinate position in her life. And so, when Dexter phoned later that night to say he was free the following evening and intended to take her out for dinner, she accepted with forced enthusiasm.

'We'll go some place really classy,' he declared, 'so get gussied up, sweetie!'

When she had replaced the receiver she remembered that all her new clothes were still out at the farm. She dialled Flint's number with a shaking hand, and when he answered almost immediately she discovered that her throat was bone dry.

'Hello!' he repeated when she didn't speak. 'Who's there?'

'It's me—Polly,' she croaked. 'I hope I'm not phoning too late.'

There was quite a pause, then he said. 'Not a bit too late, Pollyanna. As a matter of fact, I was just about to phone *you*. To discuss our schedule for the picnic on Sunday.'

'Oh, yes . . .' Her heart lifted perceptibly.

'I've only this minute returned—from a short trip.'

So *that* was why he hadn't called before. She had been a fool to feel neglected. In a voice that was a long way from her original croak she asked, 'A business or a pleasure trip?'

'Business. Purely business,' he drawled. 'I had an idea for a book on waterfalls, so I went off with Duvet to search for some. I'll tell you all about it when I see you.'

'Sounds fun!' She could have wept for joy that he was including her.

'Now—what can I do for you, Pollyanna?'

She explained that she needed some clothes, but didn't tell him what for. 'I'm pretty sure I can borrow Mom's car tomorrow, so I was wondering if I could come over.'

'Sure! No problem. I'll be here all day. Come around noon and I'll fix us lunch—like old times.' She could hear the smile in his voice.

'I'll be there,' she said, 'don't forget the mustard! Good night, Flint.'

'Good night, Pollyanna. Sweet dreams.' He hung up.

She stood for a long time in the dim hall smiling at nothing before going to the living room to ask Marjorie if she could borrow her car.

She was still in a happy mood the next morning, even though it was pouring with rain, which made driving unpleasant. 'Singin' in the rain, I'm singin' in the rain,' she bellowed lustily all the way to the Caledon Hills.

The beige stone of Crabtree Farm was stained to the colour of dark honey by the wet, and the apple trees dripped mournfully. But nothing could dampen Polly's buoyant spirits, and she drew up by the house with a flourish.

Flint was standing at the front porch. He came to the car carrying a large striped gold umbrella. 'Whew!' he exclaimed when they had run into the shelter of the house. 'It's like being back in Lake Huron!'

The remark reminded Polly of their brief lovemaking, and she grew shy. As if he sensed her mood he opened the door to the studio stairs and whistled for Duvet. 'Friend of yours come to see you!' he called, grinning as the big dog raced upstairs and threw herself at Polly with yelps of delight.

'Oh, Duvet, you *fool!*' she giggled, as Duvet put her paws on her shoulders in an effort to show her pleasure. It was hard to remain shy under such an onslaught, and she began to feel more at ease.

'You'd almost think we'd missed you,' Flint said softly, and she went pink.

'Where's Sable?' She hoped that by mentioning Sable's name she would dispel the atmosphere of intimacy that seemed to occur now when she was alone with Flint.

'She's making a TV commercial in New York.' He seemed quite casual about it. 'She got that cosmetics account, by the way. She'll be taking off for Paris soon.'

'*Great!*' Polly said heartily. She *was* pleased, of course, but the prospect of working for Flint without his lady around to make it a nice safe threesome was disturbing. 'Good for Sable. She must be very happy.'

'Happy?' Flint answered enigmatically. 'Well . . . yes. Happy about the *job*, that is.'

She couldn't stop herself asking, 'Are you happy about it?' even though she was afraid she was treading on dangerously personal ground.

'Of course I am. It's a great break for her. She deserves a break, does Sable.' Abruptly he suggested that Polly go upstairs and get her clothes while he finished making the lunch, and she felt he was making it clear he didn't want to discuss Sable any further.

Her room looked welcoming. Somebody had put a vase of field daisies on the dressing table, and she was forcibly reminded of the resplendent blossoms in the house in Toronto. These simple flowers pleased her far more.

She changed out of her 'old' clothes into her new cotton pants and a peach-coloured top before joining Flint in the kitchen.

He had lit a small fire. There was really no need for one, but the burning apple boughs smelt aromatic, and it was cheering to see the flames dancing on the kitchen walls, and bouncing off the copper cauldron that she had filled with fir-cones when she had first moved in.

'Thought we'd eat by the fire.' He put a tray of food down on a side table and lifted Fellini off one of the wing chairs where he had been contentedly purring. 'What's happened to your manners?' he said to the cat. 'Didn't I teach you always to give your seat to a lady?' Offended, Fellini stalked to the furthest edge of the hearth-rug and, turning his back, began to clean his paws elaborately.

Polly settled herself in the chair, her loose curls gleaming against the faded chintz. 'Mmm!' she murmured happily, 'this is nice.'

'Yes, it is,' he said, his voice as dark as midnight.

Warning bells started to sound faintly in Polly's head. It was happening again! That cosy, exciting intimacy the moment she was alone with him.

Perhaps if she concentrated on mundane thing—like food—she could keep the conversation on an even keel. 'What kind of sandwiches do we have?' she asked brightly.

He gave a soft laugh before replying. 'Beef, rare, with plenty of mustard, and chopped egg. Okay?'

'*Delicious!* I adore roast beef sandwiches,' she babbled. 'And chopped egg—they *complement* each other, don't you think? One bland and the other . . .'

'Shut up, darling,' said Flint, handing her the plate. 'Choose your sandwich and relax. There's nothing to worry about.'

It was all very well for him to tell her to relax. That 'darling' had started her heart pounding like a trip-hammer, and the fact that she seemed to enjoy it when he used endearments didn't help.

She laid aside the beef sandwich she had taken at random. She didn't think she was capable of swallowing anything right now. Her throat felt too tight.

'I'm having a beer, or there's chocolate milk.' He went over to the fridge.

Turning to answer, she found herself admiring his lean, hard thighs. He was wearing a pair of ancient jeans and a navy tee-shirt, the sort of garments she was sure Dexter wouldn't be caught dead in. But she thought he looked just as attractive as Dexter did, in spite of the actor's fancy wardrobe. In fact, now that she had come to know Flint, she realised that he was really very sexy. Not in an obvious, 'film star' way, but he possessed a strength, an aura of virility—and at this particular moment it was *just* what she didn't need!

'Beer or chocolate milk?' he asked again.

'Oh, chocolate milk, please. I love chocolate.'

'I remember.' He smiled at her as he placed the carton in front of her and handed her a glass.

Polly took a determined bite of her sandwich. When she had swallowed it she said, 'Now, about this picnic . . . How much equipment do you plan to take?' She hadn't the faintest idea what she was talking about, but she wanted to sound matter-of-fact.

'Now, let's see. A couple of cameras . . . a lot of film . . . and you.' His eyes were sparkling with amusement, and she cursed herself for being such a fool.

However, she persisted. 'Well—shall I meet you on the island? Or what?'

'The film company's laying on a special ferry for V.I.P.s. We're to take that. So I'll pick you up at your house at eleven. Should give us plenty of time.' He took a drink of beer. 'Having got that settled, relax and enjoy your lunch.'

She did feel easier then, for it seemed she was not to return to Crabtree Farm yet, and with Sable in New York that was a good thing. But paradoxically she felt let down. She missed the farm and Duvet—and Flint, too, an unsettling voice inside her insisted.

So she couldn't help asking, 'When do you want me to come back? I mean to do the housekeeping?'

He tapped his thumbnail against his white teeth for a moment. 'Let's see what Sable's plans are before we fix anything,' he said at last. 'I have a feeling you might feel—happier—if she were around.' He raised his eyebrows quizzically. 'Am I right?'

Flushing, she nodded and muttered something about her mother liking it if another woman was in residence, although Marjorie had never expressed an opinion on the subject. He accepted this, and by the time they had finished their lunch, and fed the scraps to Duvet, the atmosphere between them was comfortable again.

This was mostly due to Flint, who started to tell her of his trip in search of waterfalls to photograph. The old comradeliness reasserted itself, and by the time they were stacking their plates in the dishwasher she was laughing at his jokes again, her hazel eyes free from anxiety.

The old grandfather clock chimed four. 'I must go,' Polly said, wiping the tray free of crumbs. 'Thank you for lunch, and for the information on waterfalls. I think it should make a terrific book.'

'So do I.' Flint took the sponge out of her hand and spun her round to face him. 'Let's discuss it over dinner tonight. You haven't sampled our village restaurant yet, have you?'

She disengaged her hand. 'I can't. I have a date.'

'A serious date,' he smiled, 'or one that you can break? You know where the phone is.'

She answered him lightly. 'A serious one. One I can't break.'

'Okay. How about tomorrow night?'

Her caution had returned; she said, 'I can't tomorrow night, either.' If Dexter wanted to see her tomorrow night too she intended to be free. It was part of her plan to rekindle the spark.

His lips thinned. 'Are you going to free *any* night before the picnic?'

'I'm really not free for dates at all,' she told him, and when he gave her a look like blue ice she added firmly, 'I'm *committed*.

'*Committed!*' he barked. 'What the hell do you mean?'

'Don't you dare shout at me!' Her calm had deserted her and she was trembling. 'I'm committed. I'm . . .' She couldn't being herself to say 'in love', so she said instead, 'I'm *fond* of someone.'

'How nice! Anyone I know?' he asked in a voice of silky suavity which did nothing to disguise the cutting edge.

'None of your business,' she shot back. Anger was starting to flow over her like a hot tide.

'Oh, yes, it is my business! It's more of my business than you realise.' She started to leave but he caught her by the wrist. 'It's Dexter, isn't it? He's the one you're *fond* of!' He uttered the word with such withering sarcasm she flinched and pulled away from his grasp.

'Since you ask, yes, it is. Although I'm surprised someone with your—awareness—has to be told.' If he was going to fight her with sarcasm she would try and dish it out too. 'Anyone with a *modicum* of intelligence would have know that I thought Dexter Grant was *marvellous*. I never hid the fact.'

'You never hid the fact that you were a mindless groupie at the beginning,' he said with venom. 'I thought you'd progressed from that.'

'I have progressed,' she spat at him. 'I now go out on dates with him. So much for your mindless groupie!'

He went very still and she could see the fury drain out of him. 'I shouldn't have called you that,' he said. 'Mindless is the last thing you are.'

'But still a groupie,' she prompted him with bitter hilarity, 'because if that means someone who admires another person, then that's what I am.'

'It's okay to *admire* Dexter,' he said, raking his hands through his crest of red hair. 'He's a terrific actor, and a nice guy——.'

'You don't have to build him up to *me,*' she reminded him.

He went on, '—but you're not—I don't know how to say this—you're not in his league. . . .'

'Thank you *very* much!' She was so pale with temper her freckles stood out, pale discs of gold.

'No, no!' He tugged at his hair with both hands. 'I don't mean it that way. But Dexter travels in a very fast lane—it's not your style, Pollyanna. He works hard, but he plays hard too. He's inclined to drink too much and——'

'—and with friends like you he doesn't need any enemies!'

'I'm a good friend to Dexter. He knows that,' he replied with dignity. 'All I'm saying is—be careful. Don't get hurt—and don't hurt others in your relentless quest for glamour.'

'I'm not looking for glamour,' she cried, stung because when she had first met him that was exactly what she had been doing. 'It's Dexter himself I'm in . . . in . . .' Again her mouth refused to form the word, but he said it for her.

'If you're trying to tell me you're in love with Dexter I simply don't believe it.' She could see that his temper was at breaking point again. 'You hardly know him!'

'I know him better than you think!' She experienced a moment of painful triumph as she watched this shaft hit home, then, ignoring the small voice of reason at the back of her mind, she said deliberately, 'I only took the job with you because I wanted the chance to get to know Dexter.'

There was a terrible silence, during which she felt as if icy water was being poured down her back. Flint stood, as still as if he were carved out of granite. The awful moment was broken by Duvet, who whined and pushed her head up against her master's leg. He patted her, but did not take his eyes off Polly.

'Congratulations,' he said at last, 'you got what you wanted.'

'I'd better go,' she said, taking her holdall and making for the kitchen door. 'I . . . I guess you won't want me to work as your assistant now, so I'll say goodbye.'

He was across the floor in two strides, gripping her arms so that she dropped the bag on to the floor.

'We made a deal,' he grated, his white face inches from hers. 'I've fulfilled my part of it. You're damn well not going to default now. I'm picking you up at eleven as planned. You're not quitting on me!'

He gave her a none too gentle shove before calling to Duvet and heading for his office, leaving Polly to go to her car alone.

She drove back to Toronto in a raging rainstorm, but it was nothing compared to the storm in her heart. Blinking away furious tears, she peered into the deluge, wondering why on earth she had said those things. She had wanted to reawaken her first passion for Dexter, but all she had succeeded in doing was hurting Flint. For, in spite of his anger, she could tell that he was deeply hurt.

To make herself feel better she tried to justify their quarrel: she was free to go out with whomever she pleased. Just because he was at a loose end, with Sable in New York, was no reason for him to expect Polly to be at his beck and call. He had Sable, which gave him no excuse to act like a dog in the manger because Polly was attracted to his friend. She wouldn't have been surprised if he had been going to make another play for her tonight, just out of boredom. He was untrustworthy! His behaviour the moment Sable was out of the way proved that.

By this stormy train of thought she managed to whip herself into a fit of righteous indignation by the time she drove off the Expressway ramp into the city.

She dressed and made up, taking particular care with her eyes, which were still a little red, and by the time Dexter picked her up she had regained her calm, if not her spirits.

Tonight he drove a Jaguar. He seemed to have countless types of car. She discovered later that they were leased by the film company and Dexter merely borrowed them. His agent had arranged it in order to impress his many fans.

'Sweets to the sweet, honey,' he said as he presented her with a large box of chocolates. She was grateful that Marjorie was out, for even though the box was not shaped like a heart she could imagine her mother's snort of derision.

'You look real cute, sweetie,' he said, regarding her approvingly before taking her mauve shawl and wrapping it round her shoulders.

She was wearing the bleached silk with the motif of sea-shells round the neck, and she had piled her hair high on her head and fixed shell ear-rings in her ears. She knew she looked good, but her recent quarrel with Flint still echoed in her, robbing her of pleasure.

Dexter took her to the most exclusive—and expensive—restaurant in Toronto. Situated on a rise overlooking the city, it provided a spectacular view. The downtown lights glittered beneath them like a thousand spangles strewn on black velvet. And the food was magnificent: grilled truffles, anchovies baked in little puff-pastry cases, imported quail served on a bed of artichoke hearts ... but she had no appetite and ate sparingly. She even refused a portion of the restaurant's famous chocolate praline soufflé.

However, Dexter didn't seem to notice that she was subdued. He talked steadily and she nodded and smiled, her mind still back in the Caledon Hills.

In the car he suggested they 'go back to my place for a nightcap', but she pleaded fatigue.

'You could spend the night with me,' he suggested, running his hand down her throat and letting it come to rest on the generous curve of her breast.

'No, I couldn't.' She firmly removed his hand. Fancy! she thought, the famous Dexter Grant wants to go to bed with me—and I don't feel a thing!

'Don't you like me?' he murmured softly, breathing into her ear.

'Of course. But I—I don't do that sort of thing.' It sounded terribly prissy, put like that, but she didn't want to hurt his feelings by telling him the idea didn't appeal to her.

'Hey!' He pulled away and looked at her solemnly. 'I do believe you're still a virgin. How *about* that!' He made it sound as if she had three heads.

'Yes, I'm one of those,' she agreed wearily. 'Now I do think we'd better get going, Dexter. You have an early call tomorrow, you owe it to your fans to be fresh.'

This was a very clever ploy and he started the car without further argument.

Outside her house, when she thanked him for the evening, he drew her into his arms and kissed her good night. She waited for the sky to fall, the way it had when Flint had kissed her, but it didn't. Oh, it was pleasant, being kissed by Dexter Grant. His lips felt warm on hers, and he held her with practised competence, but she experienced no swooning delight at his touch.

Very disappointed, she gently drew away from his embrace and escaped into the house. 'See you tomorrow, sweetie-pie,' he called after her.

As she fell into a troubled sleep she thought she had *better* see him a lot. It was going to take longer than she had realised to recapture that state of glazed wonder she had first experienced in the company of the legendary actor.

'Damn Flint, anyway,' she muttered sleepily, for if it hadn't been for him she wouldn't be having this difficulty.

The next day she visited Dexter on the set and was introduced to his colleagues. Some of them she recognised from that first party at his house, but nobody remembered her. This time she was fashionably dressed and coiffed. Dexter made it clear that she was the new lady in his life, and his friends fawned over her. It was a far cry from that first encounter. Now they declared she was 'adorable', laughed at her jokes, and offered her innumerable cups of coffee.

That evening she and Dexter dined at his house with a select few. She was glad there were others around, because she knew if she had been alone with him he would have tried to make love to her and she would have had the inevitable tussle. Then her reluctance to head for bedroom, which he now viewed as 'quaint', would have started to irritate him, and she would have had to either sleep with him or say goodbye. And she didn't want to say goodbye to him. Not just yet.

Truth to tell, the idea of having affairs didn't really attract her, and to have one without overwhelming passion was intolerable. She just hoped the 'overwhelming passion' for Dexter would manifest itself before too long. She was playing for time.

When one of the company offered her a lift at the end of the evening she accepted at once. She had already had one struggle with Dexter when they had been alone in the billiard room; she didn't feel up to another.

'I *love* girls who play hard to get,' he had said, nuzzling her neck.

'I'm not playing a game,' she had insisted, pushing him away. 'Dexter, don't! It tickles!' And he had laughed and called her a 'clever cookie'.

But she still went to the set the following day, and ate with him in his dressing-room, and heard his lines. As long as she could keep their relationship on this level, all was well. Dexter enjoyed showing off, and she admired his genuine talent as an actor. But the emotion she was hoping for still eluded her, and now when he kissed her she found herself thinking of tactics to evade him, rather than being swept into a maelstrom of desire.

And so it went until Sunday, the day of the picnic. The weather was perfect, hot and still, the leaves hanging motionless on the trees as if carved from green jade.

Polly wore her batik dress and her straw hat, the one Flint had given her. Her new swimsuit was packed in her tote-bag, for today it would be a relief to plunge into the cold waters of Lake Ontario.

She was waiting for Flint at ten forty-five a.m., determined not to be late. It was a re-play of that first fateful morning when he had picked her up at the crack of dawn to take her to the farm. How long ago was it? Only five weeks! This morning her heart seemed to have come out of its temporary retirement and was beating fast. How would she behave when she saw him? She resolved to let him make the first move. Then she would forgive him. So she stood in the baking sunshine, a small, tense figure, her childlike lips firmly gripped to stop them trembling.

At eleven on the dot Flint's orange BMW screeched to a halt beside her. At the sight of him hunched over the wheel her heart gave such a lurch that for a moment she was incapable of movement.

She waited for his 'Good morning, Pollyanna', and his lopsided grin.

Leaning over to open the passenger door, he growled, 'Get in. We haven't got all day!' and her heart dropped like a stone.

The war was still on!

Silently she climbed in, determined now to present a front of icy dignity. To show him she didn't care if he was mad or not. The fact that she did was her own business. She had some difficulty maintaining her dignified front when she discovered Duvet in the back seat. It was hard to remain aloof when her hat was being knocked off by a frenziedly welcoming dog!

'Duvet, sit!' yelled Flint, and the dog did as she was

told, no doubt taken aback by the ferocity in his voice.

And that was the extent of their conversation on the drive down to the harbour. Insulated from each other, they sat, each stubbornly determined not to be the first to speak.

CHAPTER NINE

ORIGINALLY the Toronto Islands were known as 'The Peninsula', but a severe storm in 1858 washed away the link to the mainland, creating this haven, a short ferry ride from the city. In the dim past, five weeks ago, Polly had enjoyed taking her bike across on the ferry and exploring the large parkland. There was an animal farm, amusement rides, and an assortment of cafés on Centre Island. If she was in a more solitary mood she would cycle to Ward's Island, with its tiny community of year-round dwellings, or she would go west to Hanlan's Point, visiting the abandoned lighthouse which was said to be haunted by the ghost of a murdered lighthouse keeper on the way. Or sometimes she would rent a canoe and paddle through one of the lazy lagoons. It had always been one of her favourite places, and usually she had a feeling of holiday about her when she landed on its shores. She didn't feel that way today, not with Flint, silent and grim beside her. Even Duvet was subdued.

Today, they were taken to Centre Island, not by one of the crowded ferries where people played transistors, and hugged coolers and children, and laughed good-naturedly in the crush, but by a sleek private speed-boat hired by the film company for the occasion. It zipped past the laden public ferry with its bow in the air like a haughty duchess snubbing her neighbours.

The marquee for the picnic had been erected on an enormous meadow shaded by tall green trees. Dexter's name was printed on a banner, and a booth had been set up where he could meet the public and sign autographs. Inside the tent, a long trestle groaned under the weight of food, and an equally well-stocked bar stood at another end. Already, flocks of curious bystanders were pushing at the ropes that cordoned off the area. They were shown to a smaller tent with a private bar and a garden chair in it. Wai, Dexter's man, was hanging a towelling robe and a change of clothes on to a portable rack. When he saw Flint his dried-prune face split in a welcoming grin. 'Mr. Dexter, he be here soon,' he said, then his eye fell on Duvet at Flint's heels and the grin died. 'Mr. Dexter no like dogs,' he said. 'Maybe you should tie it up outside.'

'Don't worry about it, Wai, I'll deal with Mr. Dexter,' said Flint. 'The dog is one of the props for today.'

They left Polly's tote-bag and the camera-bag in Dexter's tent before going out into the sunshine again. 'Is it true about Duvet being a prop?' Polly asked Flint. It was the first time she had addressed a remark to him since they had met earlier.

'I'm not in the habit of telling lies,' he replied curtly.

'I merely wondered how you intended to use her. Since I'm suppsed to be your assistant it might help if I knew.'

He looked at her sourly. 'It will sell more magazines, and give Dexter a good image, if he's photographed in the company of his dog,' he said.

'But isn't that dishonest? Dexter hates dogs,' she protested.

'The world of image-making often is,' he said bleakly. 'This is an actor's profile we're shooting, not a documentary.' He scuffed at the grass with the toe of his worn running shoe and she felt a moment's pity for him. She knew how much he hated this kind of work. This was the world he was making a conscious effort to leave, but because of the commitments of friendship he was caught up in it again.

'Hi, guys!' Dexter, surrounded by a coterie of hangers-on, came towards them. 'Sorry I'm late. Got trapped on the phone talking to Sable at the airport Her plane to Paris has been delayed!'

Flint didn't comment, and Polly wondered if he had driven Sable to the airport earlier and was taking out his distress at the parting on her Anyway, she didn't care! *Dexter* was the man she was interested in, and she focused her attention on him. He did look splendid in his immaculate white trousers and scarlet shirt. His shoes were supple white leather, and two gleaming gold chains nestled on his chest. And yet . . . wasn't he just a touch *too* groomed for an island picnic? Didn't Flint, in faded khaki pants and shirt, look more attractive in his sinewy masculinity than Dexter did, for all the latter's sheen? This time Polly didn't stifle the idea, and she was surprised to discover that she found Flint physically more appealing than the handsome film star. As if to test her, Flint pulled his battered baseball cap from his hip pocket and crammed it on to his untidy red head. She still found him attractive.

'Time to get to work,' he said. 'Back up, and make your entrance again, Dexter. We might as well start with that.'

'Got to have my kiss first,' said the actor, grabbing Polly and kissing her lingeringly. 'Hello, beautiful—I've missed you.'

Flint's face remained completely expressionless. 'Make sure you have plenty of film ready, Polly. I'll be taking a lot of shots,' was his sole remark.

Dexter caught sight of Duvet and a frown crossed his handsome face. 'Did you have to bring the dog, Flint? You know how I feel about them.

'For today you're crazy about them!' Flint informed him. 'Use your talent as an actor. You will look really good at this shindig with your faithful dog at your heels.'

'He has a point, Dexter baby,' agreed a short fat man who turned out to be the actor's manager. 'Maybe we could find a child for you to kiss, too.'

Unamused, Dexter growled, 'Over my dead body! A dog's bad enough,' before retracing his steps so Flint could take pictures.

Polly pricked up her ears. So Dexter Grant disliked *children* as well as animals! Her illusions suffered another blow, and like a flashback at a movie she had a mental picture of Flint playing with Mabel's grandson. She was pretty sure, if the shoe was on the other foot, Flint wouldn't object to kissing a baby.

The public now started to crowd around and demand autographs, and Flint had soon used up his first roll of film. Duvet behaved magnificently, posing when requested, and not forcing herself on her temporary master, who ignored her unless a fan or the camera was observing him.

Lunch was handled in two shifts. The first was for the crew. A mountain of hamburgers were grilled on the park's barbeques, and soft drinks were handed out. Dexter wandered among his admirers, a hamburger in his elegant hand, Duvet salivating at his heels.

Photographs were taken while he mingled with the crowd. After a half an hour of this activity, he disappeared into his private tent, motioning Polly and Flint to follow him.

'That's enough of the peasants for a while,' he said, lying down on the lounger and dropping his hamburger to the ground, where it was snapped up by Duvet. 'Open up the champagne, Wai, and pour me a rum and orange. And get chairs for Mr Flint and Miss Polly. We'll have *our* lunch in here.'

'Thanks, Wai, but I'll settle for a hamburger outside,' said Flint; he looked irritated. 'You'd be amazed what good pictures the peasants make. I don't need you, Polly,' he went on, when Polly turned to go with him. 'Stay here and enjoy yourself. After all, that's why you took this job, isn't it?

The colour swept over her face. That *was* what she had done. As she had grown to know Flint, that first, unworthy motive had changed. But it was too late to explain that to him now.

When Flint had gone, Dexter said, 'You mustn't let old Flint get to you, he's always been kinda touchy about the "good life".'

'How do you mean, touchy?' She accepted the glass of champagne Wai handed her. She remembered Flint teasing her about drinking a lot of champagne once she was launched on a life of glamour. It was funny how being bad friends with Flint seemed to affect the taste of wine.

'Oh, he has these dumb ideas! He gave up a really good career in fashion to photograph a bunch of nobodies and *write* about them, you know.' He finished his rum and handed the glass to Wai for a refill. 'Said working in fashion *bored* him ... stuff like that. Dumb! He was making a lot of bread as a fashion photographer ... and when you're making good money who cares if you're bored or not? He's a nice guy, Flint, but a little screwy!' He smiled indulgently, waiting for her to share the joke.

'I don't agree with you, Dexter.' She tried to keep her voice firm, but it trembled slightly. 'I think Flint's *brave*—not "screwy". And very talented.' She warmed to her theme. 'The fact that he isn't taken in by what you call the "good life" is a virtue. He's too smart to be deceived by sham.' Not like me, she thought, surprised to feel the prick of tears in her eyes.

'Well, well, well!' Dexter looked at her thoughtfully. 'You sure are the loyal employee, sweetie!'

She gave a little gulping laugh. 'Yes. And talking of employees—I'd better go out there and see if I can help him. He doesn't pay me to sit around with famous film stars guzzling champagne, you know.' She made for the entrance, waiting for Dexter to object to being left to eat lunch by himself. But he merely regarded her speculatively.

Outside, while looking for Flint, she bumped into one of the assistant directors of the film, a plump young man she had met on the set, and to whom she had taken an instant dislike. Judging from the aura of whisky that hung around him, he had been visiting the bar in the marquee, and he did his best to persuade her to have a drink with him, trying to bar her way when she refused and generally behaving like a pest. However, she managed to push him aside—which wasn't difficult given his condition—and headed for the beach. She walked past the children's pool to the untended beachfront, where the water was deeper. Slipping off her shoes, she wriggled her toes in the sand, which was as dry as popcorn, and stared out over the lake. She remembered that other great lake, Lake Huron, and how Flint had floated beside the life-raft, and made her feel protected—safe. A feeling she didn't have with Dexter in his shiny, spotlit life. And it wasn't just that Flint made her feel looked-after—he made her feel she could look after *herself,* too. He gave her confidence, made her secure. And it was then, sitting gazing at the dancing water, that she suddenly understood that for weeks now she had been looking on the face of love, and had never recognised it. She had been too dazzled by the glare of the glamorous life she thought she craved.

She *loved* Flint. It was as simple as that—and *he* loved Sable. Not quite so simple after all! And while she might have learnt to assert herself and go after the things she wanted, going after other women's men was forbidden, no matter how much she might want them. Who knows, she thought glumly, when this job with Dexter is finished I'll probably never see him again, and then I shall recover from this unexpected love. But in her heart she knew that she would never recover from it. She would learn to smother it, like a banked fire, but it would never by extinguished.

She heard shouts and laughter, and the film people came down to the beach for an impromptu game of baseball, Flint and Dexter with them. Grabbing a baseball bat, Dexter struck a pose for the camera, flashing his famous smile at Polly, who stood silently watching this display.

She was scarcely aware of him, and all through the

long afternoon, while she helped Flint, and lugged the tripod and the camera-bag, and obeyed Flint's curt commands, she was lost in wonder at her discovery.

Now, when she looked at him, his baseball cap pushed back on his crest of untidy hair, his shirt open to reveal his broad chest, she wondered how on earth she could have been so blind! Her body had known. When she responded so passionately to his lovemaking, her response had been fuelled by love, not lust as she had supposed. She should have listened to her pounding blood and realised that she had found her own true love.

And what was the good of *that?* When her own true love was virtually living with somebody else! She heard a mocking echo of Flint begging Sable to stay on at Crabtree Farm. 'I need you here more than ever,' he had said. And Sable had laughed and agreed, and with a catch in his voice he had fervently blessed her. He wasn't really aware of the plump little person who had so conveniently arrived to type his manuscript. Oh, he had kissed her, but then what a great way to spend the time when you're marooned on an island! And he hadn't let it go any further because he was a decent man who didn't make a game of seducing naive girls. And he had helped her improve her appearance because he was kind and generous.

Before the sun went down, some of the party changed and went swimming in the glassy lake. There had been plans to go surf-sailing, a sport Dexter enjoyed, but the water was too calm, so they had to be content with the baseball, and an improvised game of water-polo, at which Dexter, resplendent in his silver trunks, excelled.

Flint had changed into navy trunks. He had nice lean thighs, hard and athletic. 'I'm going to wade out and take pictures,' he said, throwing his towel on to the sand. Duvet, who had been following at his heels, sat on it. 'Did you bring your bathing suit?'

Polly ventured a weak joke. 'Yes, but I don't have police protection!' But he merely frowned and said,

'Well, hurry up and get into it, or the game will be over.'

When she came back to the shore wearing her new bronze suit, Flint was already waist deep in the water taking random shots of the romping teams. As she waded out to join him, Dexter stopped leaping around—always with his best profile to the camera—and let out a wolf-whistle.

'Woweee! Get a load of that!' He started charging towards them, causing Flint, who was in the process of taking a picture, to curse as he lost focus. 'You look great, kiddo!' Dexter enthused, and, putting his hands on her naked sides, he attempted to dance her around in a circle. With a shriek she lost her balance and the two of them were submerged for a moment, then they surfaced, spluttering and creating a minor whirlpool.

Flint held his camera high over his head. 'Do you *mind*?' he said coldly. 'You'll get water all over the lens if you're not careful.' He gave Polly a baleful look. 'I'll be finished in a few minutes, then you can horse around all you want.'

'Sorry.' She pushed her dripping hair out of her eyes. She wished Dexter would stop goggling at her like that, it embarrassed her and visibly annoyed Flint.

'Get back with the others, will you, Dexter?' he said. 'This series of pictures is supposed to show you interacting with the *crew,* not with my assistant.'

But Dexter did not immediately release his hold on Polly's midriff. 'Okay, okay, don't lose your cool!' he drawled. Then, after giving her another hug, he leaned over her, so that she could smell the rum on his breath, and said softly, 'Tonight's the night, baby. You and me.'

Face flaming, Polly watched him return to his companions. Flint's expression was inscrutable. He squeezed off a few more frames and then waded back to the shore. She followed him.

'I'm calling it quits now!' he said. 'Make a note of the film used and leave my stuff in Dexter's tent. Then you're through for the day.' He could have been addressing a total stranger.

'Very well. Are you going back now . . . or what?' She felt as if she was standing on another planet rather than a foot away from his sun-gold body.

'Right now I'm going to have a swim,' he said, 'a long one. Stay, Duvet!' he ordered, and his dog sat obediently on the towel. Without a backward glance at Polly, he ran down the short sandy incline and into the waiting lake.

She watched him as he swam away from her, away from the noisy group still frolicking in the shallows. A lone figure swimming steadily along the path of light created by the setting sun, as if his destination was that crimson disc sinking in the west. Oh, Flint, I love you, she thought, I love you so much. Please let's be friends again. But even as she wished for that she knew now that friendship with Flint could only give her pain. She needed more from him than that.

Dexter came out of the water. 'You should have joined us,' he said, 'not waited for me all on your lonesome,' and she smiled wryly, since waiting for Dexter had been the last thing in her mind.

'I'm going to stay here for a bit,' she said, sitting on a grey log. 'To watch the sun go down. I'll join you presently.'

He looked mildly aggrieved. 'What's to watch?' he demanded. 'It goes down the same way every time.' But she just smiled, and with a shrug he and his friends went through the stand of aspen trees back to the marquee.

The log, worn smooth with time and weather, still held heat from the sun. The air was warm, and soon Polly's swimsuit was dry. Her hair fell softly on her shoulders, brushing her sun-warmed skin like brown silk.

Apart from one or two laggard picnickers, she was the only one left on the beach.

Flint had turned around now and was swimming back. The wake from his vigorous crawl was the only motion on the mirror-like surface of the lake. Before long she could hear the splash, splash, as he kicked at the water. The last picnicker had left when he waded out, dripping, his hair, for once, a sleek red helmet. Duvet gave a bark of welcome and ran up to meet him.

She stood up as he approached her. 'Was the water wonderful?' she asked. 'I should have gone in too, only I'm lazy.'

'Didn't you understand?' His eyes were as hard as pebbles. 'You're through for the day. You can join your— your friends now.'

The top of her head just reached his chest, which glistened with water-drops. She longed to lean against him, feel his firm flesh against her cheek. 'They're your friends, too,' she said.

'*Dexter's* my friend ... and, right now, three's a crowd,' he replied.

'Rubbish! Besides, it's a party,' she pleaded.

'I'm not in a party mood.' Turning away from her he picked up his towel and started to dry himself. It was a dismissive gesture, and with a heavy heart she left him.

Before she reached the tent, where she had left her clothes, an unpleasant incident occurred. The young assistant director, now much the worse for drink, staggered out of the bushes, nearly falling on top of her.

'Watch it!' exclaimed Polly, stepping back to avoid contact. But the man had other ideas.

'You sexy li'l thing,' he slurred, lurching towards her. 'Gimme a kiss.' He grabbed her by one shoulder, muttering something about the shape of her breasts.

Infuriated rather than scared, Polly jabbed her elbow as hard as she could into the soft swell of his belly. He gave a gasp and stepped backwards, clutching his pot. 'Li'l *bitch*!' His red eyes glared like an angry wart-hog. 'You li'l bitch!' Then he gave a cry of surprise as Flint, who had come up behind them, lifted him bodily by the collar of his shirt and pitched him back into the bushes where he lay, gasping with amazement.

'Get lost, creep!' Flint told him through gritted teeth,

'and if I catch you bothering her again I'll break you arm!' Duvet gave a couple of menacing barks for good measure before Flint called her sharply to heel.

'Thanks,' said Polly with a shaky smile, 'you're a regular knight in shining swim trunks!'

'You seem capable of taking care of yourself,' he said, and she saw that he was still trembling with anger. 'That's good. If you're going to play with the crocodiles it's as well to develop a few teeth.' He looked so forbidding that she didn't try to thank him again, and they walked silently back to the marquee where the party was in full swing.

Dexter was holding court at the bar. When he saw Flint and Polly he came to them, holding the inevitable glass in his hand. 'C'mon and have a drink,' he invited, with the bonhomie of one who had had a couple already. He reached out to draw Polly closer, but she evaded him.

'I want to change, I'll be back in a minute,' she promised.

'Well, I wanna' have a word with Flint in private,' he said. 'But don't be too long, sweetie, I've missed you.' He smiled at her fondly as she escaped to the other tent.

Pulling her dress over her head, she resolved to tell him tonight that she could never feel anything more than friendship for him. She wasn't looking forward to the interview, but it had to be done. It was only fair to Dexter, and she knew she couldn't bear to have him touch her and kiss her, not when she loved Flint so much. And she also knew that Dexter wasn't going to be content with just kissing much longer. His remark about tonight being 'the night' still rang ominously in her ears.

Using the mirror that had been propped up on a trestle, she hastily pinned up her hair, which had dried in a mass of curls since her dunking. Her skin glowed from a day in the open air, and even though the sprinkling of freckles on her retroussé nose were more noticeable now, she thought she didn't look too bad.

There was no sign of Flint when she returned to the

marquee. Dexter was standing at the bar. He gestured to her to join him, and when she did he put a possessive arm round her waist. 'What d'you wanna' drink, sweetie?' he asked. 'Anything you fancy—you jus' name it.' He smiled at her expansively, his grey eyes slightly out of focus.

'What I'd really like is something to eat,' she told him, and when he started to protest she explained, 'I didn't get any lunch today.'

Wai had returned to the city, but a henchman was dispatched to find food, and while she waited she sipped some white wine which she drowned in soda water, for she intended to keep a clear head for her talk with Dexter. Although she was beginning to wonder if he was going to be in any state to take in what she had to tell him. However, he didn't seem to be much the worse for his excesses, for apart from the occasional blurred speech, and a vagueness in his eyes, he seemed in control—so far! She just hoped the party wouldn't go on too long. Although it didn't show any signs of finishing yet. The tent was packed, and smoky, and noisy.

When she could make herself heard over the din she asked where Flint was. 'Gone home, sweetie,' Dexter replied. 'Just as well, too, he sure was crabby!' Crabby or not, she knew she would rather be with him than with any member of this glittering crowd! The party surged around her. The rich and famous, drinking, and laughing, and shouting witticisms at the tops of their voices. Sipping her wine, Polly observed them. Some wore outlandish costumes. One well-known actor had a live cockatoo perched on his shoulder. It regally accepted peanuts from time to time, and added an occasional squawk to the general cacophany.

She began to notice that the eyes of most of the guests were never still. While they laughed and joked they were always looking about them, as if they were afraid of missing the one person they *really* wanted to impress. The one person who might further their careers. It was like being surrounded by a dozen cabaret acts. Everybody was performing. All at once she felt very sorry for them. How sad to be compelled to always put on a show. To have to glitter and sparkle, and never be able to relax and simply *be yourself*. What an empty, lonely life.

That was what Flint had tried to tell her. He had recognised the shallowness behind the hype and had turned his back on it, because he was far too genuine for such a vapid world. And he had been right! All it took to be accepted here was a good haircut and a couple of fashionable outfits. And all *that* required was money! Well, she had learnt something. She had learnt that this world wasn't for her either—the price was too high.

When her sandwich arrived, Dexter suggested she take it to his tent. 'I've got some champagne on ice there,' he told her, 'an' we can be alone. I haven't seen you alone all day, sweetie.'

She agreed, for this seemed like a good opportunity to tell him that apart from the business of the photo-story she wouldn't be seeing him again.

He seated her in the garden lounger, and after pouring a flute of champagne for her and a rum and orange for himself, came and sat on the end of the chair. 'I've given Wai instructions to leave us a cold buffet and then take the night off, sweetie,' he told her, 'so you don't really need that crummy sandwich, do you?' He took the paper plate out of her nerveless hand and smiled at her with fuddled prurience. 'The night is our, honeychild!'

'It isn't, actually,' said Polly, as crisply as she could. 'I have to—to talk seriously to you, Dexter . . .'

'You don't have to say anything, sweetie.' He chuckled fatuously. 'Jus' lie back and enjoy!'

A mild panic started to grip her. She had no experience in dealing with amorous drunks, and she wasn't sure how to handle this situation. 'I can't come back with you to your place, Dexter.' She remembered how any appeal to his ego had usually worked in the past. 'For one thing, I probably have an early call to help Flint with your photo-story—but that's not——'

'There's not goin' to be any story,' he said. 'That's what I was telling Flint while you were changing.'

She was stunned. 'Wh . . . what do you mean?'

He went over to the bar, but this time he didn't re-fill his glass, but merely topped it up with juice. 'Gotta drive,' he said by way of explanation.

But Polly wasn't interested in his sudden quest for sobriety. 'What do you *mean*, no story?' she persisted.

'The dates on my play in London have been changed,' he said. 'I have to fly to England tomorrow.' He returned to her and perched himself precariously beside her. 'An' you're coming with me. It's my little surprise.' He tried to kiss her but she ducked her head. 'Now don't you worry about a thing. I've already told Flint. . .'

'You've what!' Horrified, she leapt to her feet, sending him ignominiously to the ground. 'Just *what* have you told Flint?' she demanded.

Her unexpected reaction seemed to act like a cup of black coffee on Dexter, for he appeared far more sober when he replied, 'I simply told him you'd be coming to England with me, and to forget about the photo-story. What's the matter with that?'

'The matter?' She looked at him wildly. 'In the name of all that's holy, Dexter, don't you think of *anybody* but yourself? Why did you let Flint take all those shots today if you knew you were going away? I presume you've known about this change of plans for some time?'

'A couple of days,' he admitted, climbing to his feet and brushing at his white trousers, 'but it slipped my mind. Besides, I thought it would be kinda fun to surprise you this way. If I'd told Flint he might have let the cat out of the bag.'

'*Surprise me!*' Polly groaned, and when he looked at her blankly she raged, 'how *dare* you assume I'd trot after you, without even being consulted? And how dare you tell Flint that? What will he think of me now?' Her wide-set eyes filled with a rush of tears. 'Oh, Dexter, what have you done?' she quavered. 'He'll *never* speak to me after this!'

He looked at her thoughtfully. Then he asked, 'Would that be so terrible?'

'Yes ... yes ... except ...' The tears slid down her cheeks.

'You love him, don't you, sweetie?' he said softly. 'You're in love with Flint.'

Miserably, all her anger dissipated, she nodded. 'I didn't know until today,' she said. 'I was going to tell you tonight—but I never got the chance. I'm—I'm sorry, Dexter—I——'

'Forget it!' he said tersely, handing her a crisp linen handkerchief. 'I suppose I should have guessed. You defended him like crazy if I so much as made a remark about any of his nutty ideas.'

'His ideas aren't nutty,' she said, dabbing at her eyes.

'You see! You're at it again.' He returned to the bar and this time he did add rum to his drink. 'Does he know?'

She paled visibly. 'Heavens, no! He thinks I'm in love with you. And at first I thought I was—only ...'

'Thanks a bundle,' he grimaced, and when she whispered 'Sorry, Dexter,' he went on. 'Forgive me if I don't turn cartwheels, but any guy's ego takes a beating when the chick he's been lusting after turns out to have fallen for his best friend.'

'And you're not just "any guy", are you?' she said with a watery smile.

He bowed his head in acknowledgement and then smiled at himself. 'True! But I'll recover. Anyway you don't have any reason to cry, sweetie. All you have to do is tell him how you feel, and take it from there.'

'What good would that do?' She folded his hankie and handed it back to him. 'He's in love with Sable. The reason he's so morose is because she's away.'

Dexter's handsome grey eyes opened wide. 'Flint and Sable!' he exploded, 'are you *crazy?* I've known both of them for years, I'd know if there was something between them. They're just friends, good friends, that's all.'

'*Very* good friends,' Polly said grimly. 'Did you know that Sable's been living at Flint's farm?'

'So that's where she was,' he said. 'I tried to call her at her apartment a couple of times but couldn't get her.'

'You see?'

But Dexter refused to be convinced. 'It doesn't prove a thing,' he insisted. 'I tell you I *know* those two. There's nothing between them except friendship. Anyway, I'll be seeing Sable in England. I'll ask her myself.'

Since just talking about Flint's attachment to Sable was like twisting a knife in her heart, Polly didn't pursue this. Picking up her tote-bag, she held out her hand and said, 'Goodby, Dexter. It's been wonderful knowing you. And thank you for being so understanding.'

The actor pursed his lips. 'Do I have a choice?' he enquired bitterly, and when she smiled he added, 'do you mind finding your own way home, sweetie? I think I'll stay here for a bit ... drown my sorrows.' He looked at her tragically, but she knew that it was really his vanity that was suffering, and she suspected that he was beginning to enjoy the role of disappointed lover, and intended to play it to the hilt. She left him sitting in the garden lounger, a fresh glass of rum in his hand, and she wouldn't have been surprised to hear him quoting poetry to himself as she walked away.

Polly felt very unhappy as she stood at the rail of the crowded ferry watching the lights of the city come closer. The smaller buildings looked like squat little trolls crouching beside the newer, taller ones. The air was cool on her sunburnt cheeks, but she derived no pleasure from this. It was all very well for Dexter to say he would have known if they were lovers, she had had ample proof that when it came to noticing things that were not directly connected with him, the handsome actor was not particularly perceptive. Besides, he hadn't overheard Flint begging Sable to stay on—she had.

And now Flint thought she was off to England, like a
regular camp follower, or, as he had so unkindly referred
to her, a 'groupie'.

Well, she could do something about that! She could
phone him and let him know that she hadn't gone
traipsing off to Europe with the first man who asked her.
Not that he probably gave a damn, but it would make *her*
feel better. It would be a small salve for her pride. In any
case, she supposed she was still technically his employee,
and it was only right she should let him know that she
was still available if he wanted her to continue working
for him. Except that she couldn't do that. Not now. That
was more than she could bear. And from the cold way he
had treated her all day she was pretty sure he wasn't
interested in having her around.

The boat came into the dock, and the moment the
broad steel gangplank had been dropped, the crowd
swarmed forward, Polly with them, all reluctantly
making their way home after a day on the Island Park.
Standing in the subway train, pressed against the other
hot, tired passengers, she made up her mind to phone the
minute she got home. She wouldn't let this sick feeling of
apprehension every time she thought of Flint's unfriendly voice at the end of the line stop her. She would make it
short and businesslike, but at least he would get the
message that she wasn't off on some hare-brained
holiday at Dexter's expense. Perhaps that would take
some of the ice out of his voice.

But when she entered the house, the first thing she
heard was Marjorie talking on the telephone. And from
the sound of it, it promised to be a long session. The hall
light was on and her mother was surrounded by a
moutain of loose-leaf notes and paper-clippings. When
she saw Polly her eyebrows raised slightly in surprise,
and putting her hand over the mouthpiece she said in an
undertone,

'You're early! I didn't expect you for hours yet.'

Polly muttered something about being tired, then she

asked, 'Are you going to be long, Mom?'

'Yes, I am,' Marjorie said decisively, 'I'm trying to organise a rally to protest about the hiring of a man to run the new Sewage Treatment Plant.' She transferred her attention back to the phone. 'No, no woman has actually *applied* for the post,' she admitted, 'but that's not the point. . .'

Wearily, Polly made her way upstairs. She knew that Marjorie would be glued to the phone for the next couple of hours, and nothing short of a three-alarm fire would budge her. Her own phone call to Flint would have to wait till morning. Perhaps that was just as well. By then he might be more reconciled to Sable's absence and be in a better mood. And a good night's sleep would no doubt help her to maintain a normal approach when she spoke to him. Right now she was so tired that if he was short with her she was liable to burst into tears, which would be dreadful. At least, she reflected as she curled into a ball in her narrow bed, she could cry all she liked alone in her room without having to explain herself to anyone. But she was too emotionally drained to do more than shed a couple of tears before sleep claimed her, and for a few hours at least she was unconscious of the ache in her heart.

CHAPTER TEN

BEFORE Marjorie's car had backed out of the driveway the following morning, Polly dialled Flint's number. It rang for a long time, then she hung up. She tried again later in the morning, and then at hourly intervals, but always without success. The bell merely buzzed mockingly in her ear. Flint was either not answering his phone, which was unlikely since he relied on the phone for work, or he was out. To keep herself from screaming with frustration she decided to weed the back garden, ferociously yanking up dandelions as if they were bitter enemies, but this activity made her more impatient than ever and after an hour she gave up and retreated to the kitchen. Here she baked two loaves of bread and several batches of cookies between fruitless trips to the telepone. By the time Marjorie came home from work, the house was fragrant with the scent of baking, and Polly was a nervous wreck. Not wanting to draw attention to herself, she maintained an outward show of calm, only jerking like a puppet any time her mother made a move in the direction of the phone.

'Are you all *right*, Poll?' Marjorie enquired, when her daughter asked for the fourth time if she needed the phone that evening. 'You're as jumpy as a flea!'

'I'm fine,' lied Polly, taking a lemon pudding from the fridge and serving it. 'I just need the phone for a bit tonight, that's all.' She gave her mother a wide smile in an effort to appear at ease, but Marjorie wasn't fooled.

'Is it that actor who's making you behave like a scalded cat?' she asked sharply. 'I hoped you had more sense.'

'It's a *business* call,' Polly informed her loftily. 'And for your information, Dexter's gone to England and out of my life!'

'Thank God for that!' Marjorie ate a spoonful of pudding, than, noticing Polly's wistful eyes, she went on in a gentler tone, 'he wasn't for you, Poll. Believe me! You mustn't brood.'

The unaccustomed softness in her mother's manner nearly induced Polly to tell her the real reason for her depression, but at the last minute she balked. After all, there was nothing really to tell. Nothing but the poignant fact that she loved her boss, and that he loved someone else. Not exactly a unique situation, but no less painful because of its banality. Besides, she could imagine Majorie's stringent comments and she didn't feel up to coping with them at the moment.

'When you've made your call, why don't we go to a

film?' Marjorie suggested, 'There's a good comedy playing at the Rialto.'

Polly agreed, although she really didn't want to, but she knew her mother was making an effort to cheer her up, and she was grateful to her. Besides, it looked rather suspicious spending the entire evening trying to make a 'business' call. But before they left she tried again to get through to Crabtree Farm, and again she met with no success.

It was the same story when they came home from their film. And all the next day. Then, on the third morning, she received a letter. The moment she saw it lying on the mat and recognised Flint's untidy handwriting, her heart started to beat so painfully she almost cried aloud. She stood looking down at the square envelope for several seconds before taking it in her shaking hand and carrying it to the kitchen, where she placed it on the kitchen table. For some unfathomable reason, she washed her hands and removed her apron before taking a paring knife and slitting the envelope. A cheque fluttered to the ground, but she ignored it. With trembling fingers she smoothed open the accompanying sheet of thick cream paper.

'Dear Polly,' she read, 'You won't receive this until you return from England, but no doubt it will still be useful. As you already know, the photo-story on Dexter has been cancelled. However, you are entitled to a month's salary, which is the time I had allotted for the project, and I have added three months' severance pay. Our bargain is now discharged. Good luck in the future. Flint.'

She read this unfriendly letter through several times, vainly hoping to discover a grain of kindness which would nourish her aching heart, but there was none. The term 'severance pay' kept coming off the page and dancing in front of her. She remembered the dictionary definition of severance—'To put or keep apart. To break off a relationship'—and her large tawny eyes filled with tears that spilled down her cheeks. Putting her head in her hands, she let her misery overwhelm her and sobbed hopelessly for some time. 'That's enough of that!' she told herself at last, drying her eyes on a dish towel. 'Pull yourself together, girl. You're not the first one to feel this way!' That made her think of her mother, broken-hearted and pregnant with Polly, and she wept again in sympathy. Little wonder that Marjorie was abrasive sometimes; Polly had always known that her mother's cynical view of romantic matters was really an armour, but she had never understood the degree of pain before. She found a tissue in the pocket of her jeans and, blowing her nose, made a determined effort to stop crying. Crying wouldn't solve anything, besides, she had her pride. She wouldn't let on to *anyone* how unhappy she was inside. She would keep it to herself, and she wouldn't let this heartache sour her outlook on life either. The pain would dull in time. She knew it would never really leave her, but it would become blunted, and in the meantime she would create a life for herself, so that Flint, if ever he knew or cared, would be proud of her. Even more important, she would be proud of *herself*.

She reached down and retrieved Flint's cheque, and then she blinked hard, unable at first to believe what she read. It was about three times the amount she had expected. Surely he had added a zero too many? But the written amount tallied. He might be dismissing her, but he was being generous about it. More than generous! If only he had known, money was the last thing she wanted from him . . . but she mustn't indulge in that kind of thinking any more, and with set lips she carefully folded the cheque and replaced it in the envelope. An idea started to form in her head while she tidied the house, and at noon she changed into her cotton pants and tied her lustrous curls into a top-knot. Then she put the cheque into her straw bag and headed downtown.

By the time Marjorie came home that evening Polly was a registered student at the City College, taking a full course in Gourmet Cooking in the coming term. She had also found herself a part-time job waitressing in a restaurant, to augment the little that remained from Flint's generous cheque.

Over coffee she told her mother of her plans. She had expected an argument, but to her surprise Marjorie didn't give her one, and she thought she saw a gleam of respect in the older woman's eye.

'Taking the bull by the horns, are you, Poll?' was all she said, and when Polly smiled she added, 'well, I can't say I'm pleased, but one has to go after what one wants in this life. I'm glad you've learnt *that* at last.'

'Sometimes the thing you want is out of reach,' said Polly, thinking of Flint.

'The important thing is not to admit defeat,' her mother told her.

'There are moments when one must admit defeat with dignity.' She looked away then, for she was filled with such hopeless longing she was afraid her face would give her away.

'Life goes on, Poll,' her mother said softly, 'and we survive. I know, I've been there.'

Polly forced herself to look at her mother, willing her pain to stay hidden. 'I know, Mom,' she said. 'And I have an idea now what it cost you.' On an impulse she leaned across and kissed her mother's cheek. 'I think you're the greatest!' she murmured. She felt the prick of tears, then went on hurriedly, 'And now, before we drown in syrup, let's get those dishes washed.' Grumbling, Marjorie agreed. But there was a closeness between the two women that had been missing before.

The days passed with agonising slowness for Polly. She started her job in the restaurant and was glad that it tired her, for it helped to keep her mind off her unhappiness. She managed to maintain a smiling face, and to see her joking with customers, her lovely eyes bright, you would never have guessed at the ache she felt in the place where her heart used to be. The only time she allowed her guard to drop was when she was safely in bed with the light out.

Then she would quietly cry herself to sleep, to dream of Flint, and their brief, wonderful time marooned on the island.

During her waking hours, when she was waiting on tables, or doing chores around the house, she was sometimes filled with such longing for him that she almost cried out from the pain. During this time she learnt what the phrase 'a broken heart' really meant. She also learnt that a broken heart doesn't kill you . . . you just wish it would.

Her birthday came and went. She had vaguely hoped Flint would remember it and send her a card perhaps, or phone her, but of course he didn't, and apart from letters from her relatives in England and a subscription to a new feminist magazine from Marjorie, the day passed uneventfully.

She lived in this lonely hell for almost three weeks— although to Polly it seemed more like three years—when one night, as they were about to go to bed, the phone rang in the hall. Polly's heart leapt, as it always did these days when the phone rang, but in the next instant it plunged again into its frozen state, for hope was now simply a reflex action. She knew Flint would never call her.

'Get it, Poll, will you?' her mother called from the bathroom where she was brushing her teeth. 'It's probably the Women's Protest Committee for me.'

Dutifully Polly ran downstairs and picked up the receiver. There was silence on the other end of the line for a moment, and the Sable's voice came through. Polly was so surprised she nearly forgot to answer when Sable asked for her.

'Is that you, Polly?' the model repeated.

'Yes . . . Where are you, Sable?' Polly asked breathlessly.

'I'm in London.'

'London, *England*?'

'Where else? I'm in Dexter's hotel suite, as a matter of

fact. We've just come in from a disco. He says "hello",' Sable giggled.

'Oh! Say hello from me,' Polly said, wondering how soon Sable would mention Flint. Because she must be phoning Polly to find out where he was. She probably didn't know that Polly no longer worked for him. A stab of pain shot through her and she steeled herself to tell Sable without sounding upset.

'I'm phoning because Dexter tells me you think Flint and I are having an affair,' Sable went on.

'Polly, who is it?' Marjorie's voice called from upstairs, and, putting her hand over the receiver, Polly answered 'It's for me, Mom!' She turned back to the phone. 'Well—it's none of my business . . .' she muttered, 'but . . .'

'Oh, Polly *darling!*' Sable's laugh floated over the miles. 'Flint and I are just very good friends. He's my *best* friend, in fact—but it's *you* he's mad about. Didn't you know?'

Polly clung to the telephone table for support. 'Wh—what?' she croaked.

'He's *in love with you*! Has been for ages. And now Dexter tells me you feel the same way about him.'

Polly's heart started to beat harder, but this time it was from excitement, not from pain. 'Sable, are—are you *sure*?' she breathed.

'Of course I'm sure. He went *on* about you—very boring——'

'But why didn't he *say* something?'

Sable's voice suddenly went hard. 'You were otherwise occupied . . . or so it seemed to us,' she said.

'Oh, lord!' said Polly. 'What a fool I've been!'

'But you're not, are you, Poll? Otherwise occupied, I mean?' Sable was now speaking so softly Polly had difficulty hearing her.

'With Dexter? No! That was just—I was infatuated for a bit, that's all.'

There was a long sigh at the other end of the line.

'Because I have to know for sure—it's very important to me.'

Astounded, Polly said, 'You mean—you and *Dexter*! But why did you stay out on the farm all the time?'

'I can't explain now,' Sable whispered, 'Dexter's only in the next room, he'll hear me.'

'But . . .'

'I've got to hang up now,' said Sable. 'But I wanted to put you straight. I know you didn't plan it that way, but you did me a favour, ditching Dexter like that. His ego's wounded. and I'm here to put him together again. Maybe he'll finally come to his senses and recognise someone who loves him for himself and not because he's famous!'

'Oh, Sable—I'm sorry,' said Polly, remembering Sable's tragic face at the airport, when Dexter had made such a public fuss. 'I had no idea.'

'Forget it! It doesn't matter now. See you,' said Sable, and there was a click at the end of the line. Polly stood for a while listening to the dialling tone before replacing the receiver on its cradle.

She hugged herself tight in the darkness, whispering, 'He loves me! He *loves* me!' Because surely it must be true. Sable wouldn't say a thing like that if it wasn't true. She went over that brief—frustratingly brief—conversation again. 'He's in love with you . . . Has been for ages.' But why then had he begged Sable to stay on at the farm? She would have to wait till she could ask him that question. Oh, she couldn't wait to see Flint! To tell him how she felt and what a stupid mess she'd made of things. And then everything would be all right. Everything would be *wonderful*! She would explain, and he would take her in his arms. . .

'Polly! Are you coming to bed or not?' Marjorie stood at the head of the stairs, wrapped in a cotton dressing gown.

Polly unclasped her arms and, coming to the foot of the stairs, smiled into the gloom. 'Not just yet, Mom,' she said. 'I'm going to have a—a glass of wine, and sit in the garden for a bit. It's a lovely night.' She could have added, 'And I couldn't sleep if I did go to bed because my heart's too full of happiness,' but she didn't.

'Well, just don't forget tomorrow's a working day.' Her mother sounded suspicious.

Polly trilled, 'I won't. Good night, darling!' and happily scampered into the kitchen for her wine.

She sat in the little garden for a long time, and it seemed to Polly as if the stars had never shone so brightly, nor had the air caressed her skin as sweetly as it did this night. She hugged her joy close, like a cloak about her body, and the rustling trees, and the pale flowers glowing in the darkness, seemed to share in her new-found happiness. When she finally went to bed, she fell asleep at once. And her last conscious thought was 'He loves me!'

The magic was still there when she awoke in the morning. Because she was working shift-hours she left the house later than her mother, and the minute Marjorie was gone Polly phoned the farm in order to talk to Flint. She didn't know what she was going to say, but she was determined to see him. Even if it meant going out to Crabtree Farm and sitting on the doorstep until he agreed to talk to her. She was so adamant about this that it was a tremendous let-down when Mabel answered the phone.

'Flint? Oh, didn't you know, lovey, he's gone away for a bit,' Mabel said.

Polly's heart stopped singing. 'Gone away! For how long, Mabel?'

'I don't know for sure. Some weeks, he said. He took Duvet and just drove off at the crack of dawn. Really took me by surprise, he did. I come in to feed the cat and keep the place tidy, like. It's lucky you caught me.'

'Yes . . . yes. And you've no idea at *all* when he'll be back?' Polly persisted.

'Not really. But he did arrange to phone me a day or so before he arrives, so I can get in some groceries and stuff.

I'm surprised he didn't tell you, lovey,' Mabel went on.

'We . . . we had a bit of a falling out,' Polly explained, and surprisingly Mabel chuckled and said, 'A lovers tiff, eh?'

'I want to make it up with him,' said Polly. 'Do you think you could let me know when he phones? I'd like to give him a welcome home dinner as a surprise.'

'Course I will, lovey,' agreed the older woman. 'I've always fancied myself as Cupid's little helper.'

'But don't let him know, will you?' urged Polly, alarmed that in her enthusiasm Mabel might be indiscreet.

'I won't breathe a word,' Mabel promised. 'Now, you'd better give me your number, and I'll call you as soon as I hear.' Polly did this, and after a few more pleasantries had been exchanged, they said goodbye.

She felt very deflated now that she couldn't see Flint. Deflated and at a loose end, so it was really a good thing that she suddenly became aware of time and had to rush in order to get to the restaurant.

During the day she began to realise that this enforced separation might not be altogether bad. It would give her time to think about *how* she was going to tell Flint that she loved him. The longer they were apart the happier he would be to see her, so surely she would be able to sweep aside any doubts he might have without any trouble at all.

But the days still passed slowly, and she had to constantly control herself not to call Mabel. She passed her free time reading cookery books and planning the surprise dinner for Flint. She took some of the money she had earned in tips and got her thick brown hair trimmed so that it fell again in feathery curls around her face. And she indulged in a new blusher to heighten the apricot tone that the sun had given to her milky complexion. She got in touch with some of her old girl-friends, and after much teasing about her long neglect, she met them for the odd movie or ice-cream soda, downtown. And all the

while she had the feeling of being suspended in time;
waiting for the phone to ring.

Then, four weeks later, on a sunny Friday morning,
her waiting was over. Mabel called to say that Flint
would be home the following day.

'If you come in on the early morning bus I'll pick you
up in the truck and drive you out to the farm,' Mabel
suggested. 'We could go shopping for groceries first.'

'Yes . . . Oh, yes! . . . Terrific!' agreed Polly, who was
having trouble speaking. 'See you then.'

The rest of the day passed in a dream. She went to
work and arranged to take the weekend off. In the
evening after supper she washed her hair and did her
nails. She dithered over what to wear in the morning,
changed her mind half a dozen times, and generally
drove herself and Marjorie mad. Finally she lay on her
bed and tried to read one of her romances, liberated from
the shoe-box under the bed and now openly displayed on
a special bookshelf. But even this favourite pastime
failed to soothe her, so she joined her mother downstairs
and attempted to watch television.

In the morning Marjorie drove her daughter to the bus
station before going off to a weekend conference in
Ottawa. Polly had told her that Flint was coming back,
and that she was going to cook him a meal. She had not
told her just how important his homecoming was, but
neither had she pretended that this was part of her old
job. 'I want to do something nice for him, Mom,' she had
said, and Marjorie had nodded, her only comment being,
'Better him than that actor.'

Mabel was waiting at the bus stop as promised and the
two women went shopping. Polly had decided to serve a
simple meal, but one she remembered Flint particularly
enjoyed: Steak Diane, french-fried potatoes and a salad,
followed by a pudding of apricots served with a dish of
Crème Anglaise. She wouldn't have to worry about the
timing, which was a good thing since Flint had merely
said he would be arriving 'some time after lunch'.

Everything except the steak and potatoes could be cooked ahead.

As they jolted along the road in Mabel's old truck, Polly remembered her first drive out to Crabtree Farm. Then she had been coming to face the unknown, and now, with every revolution of the wheels, she felt as if she were coming home. It had been the beginning of summer then, and now summer was nearly over, the trees' thick foliage would soon become brilliant scarlet or gold in a blaze of Canadian colour. 'Like a promise fulfilled,' Polly thought, hugging herself with secret joy at the thought of the happiness ahead.

The farm seemed very quiet standing there on its hill, with no Duvet barking a welcome, and no tall figure with a crooked grin to greet her, but she and Mabel were soon busy opening windows, and shaking rugs, polishing silver, and sweeping out the kitchen, so that in no time at all the charming old house regained its comfortable 'lived-in' atmosphere.

Before she left, Mabel went to make up the bed in the master-bedroom. 'Shall I make up your room, lovey?' she asked Polly, who was filling a silver bowl with late-blooming snapdragons. 'Will you be staying the weekend?'

Polly flushed as pink as the flower she was holding. 'I don't—that is—don't bother, Mabel. I can do it,' she flustered, thinking that if she did stay the weekend perhaps she wouldn't be sleeping in her old blue and white room, and as if she could read her thoughts, Mabel gave her an understanding smile before going to get the sweet-scented linen from the closet.

After the truck had swayed down the drive, leaving Polly alone, she stopped her energetic tasks for a little while and listened to the sounds of late summer mingling with the whispers of the old house. Every sound was like a welcome. The apple tree outside the kitchen door creaked in a gentle breeze, and the monotonous call of a Red Cardinal, a bird that always reminded Polly of a

type of Canadian parrot, sounded down in the orchard.
The cat door opened and Fellini stalked in, winding
himself round her legs in a brief welcome before going to
his cat dish to demand his lunch. She opened a tin of cat
food.

'Here you are, cupboard love,' she smiled as she set the
dish back on the floor. 'Now leave me in peace. I've got
to get ready for your master.'

She didn't even make a cup of coffee for herself, for she
was too wound up now to eat or drink anything. She
carried her holdall up to her old room and, taking out her
ash-coloured dress, laid it carefully on the bed. Then she
drew the water for a bath. She threw lots of scented bath
salts into the water and clambered out of her jeans and
sweatshirt.

Standing naked in the bathroom to pin up her hair, she
looked critically at herself in the steam-misted mirror.
She would never tan, she hadn't the kind of skin that
could take the sun, but summer had given her flesh a
faint apricot blush. It also emphasised her freckles, but
that couldn't be helped; besides, Flint seemed to like
them.

After her bath she dried herself slowly on one of the big
bath towels and then, dropping it to the floor, she turned
round before the full-length glass. It reflected back a
small girl, plump and rosy as an eighteenth-century
shepherdess, with full, firm breasts, dimpled buttocks
and a gently rounded stomach. It was not the body of a
model, and never would be. But she knew now that she
was desirable, and this knowledge gave her the assurance
of beauty. When she surrendered to her lover she would
be proud of her body. Proud of her womanliness.

After she had carefully lined her eyes, and put her hair
up in a Victorian top-knot to compliment the lines of her
rose-sprigged dress, she went downstairs again. The
heels of her white pumps clicked on the polished hall
floor. Now the house seemed uncannily quiet, as if, like
its sole occupant, it was holding its breath, waiting for

the sound of a car coming up the drive. Restlessly she prowled from room to room, rearranging a flower here, straightening an ornament, smoothing the faded chintz cushions. Finally, unable to bear the suspense any longer, she went back to the kitchen and, wrapping herself in one of Mabel's large aprons, she began to mix a sponge cake.

She had just put it into the oven when Flint's orange BMW drove into the yard. She remained motionless by the stove, the shapeless apron hiding her pretty dress, a smudge of flour on her nose. All her careful plans to greet him had vanished with the sound of the car. She was paralysed. All she could do was stand and stare at the door, and when she heard his step she felt as if her heart was being drawn out of her.

He froze in the doorway. 'What are *you* here?' he asked curtly.

At the sound of his voice life flowed back into her. 'I'm baking a cake,' she said, unfastening the apron, 'to welcome you home.' She was trembling with happiness. Kiss me soon, my darling, she thought. Please, *please* kiss me.

'I sent you a cheque,' he said, his eyes as cold as Polar ice. 'Didn't you get it?'

'Yes—I——'

'Wasn't it enough?'

She blinked at him across the chasm that seemed to be opening up between them. 'Of course it was. In fact I've——'

'Why are you here, then? I don't understand.' He came into the kitchen and dumped his zipped travelling bag down on the floor with an aggresive thud.

'I told you.' She felt a horrible tightening in her throat. 'I came to welcome you home.'

'Touching!' Flint looked down into her anxious face. 'Incidentally, aren't you supposed to be in England? With Dexter?'

She almost laughed aloud with relief. Of *course*! He

didn't know that she and Dexter were finished—had never started, really. That was why he was being so hostile.

'I didn't go to England. Dexter got it all wrong.'

'That's not the way I heard it.' He pulled off his linen jacket and dropped it on to a kitchen chair. She noticed that his tan was a deeper gold, but his face looked tired in spite of his healthy colour.

'You didn't give anybody a chance to tell you differently. You left town rather fast.' Polly smiled, but he continued looking at her as if she were a stranger, and her smile faded.

'It's got nothing to do with me whether you go trailing off to England or not,' he said.

'I think it has.' He didn't reply, and she went on, 'I spoke to Sable. *She* said it mattered to you——' his face was an expressionless mask '—whether I went to to England or not.'

'Sable has a big mouth,' he said at last.

'Isn't it true, then?' she asked, in a voice barely above a whisper.

A muscle twitched in his cheek, then he pulled his khaki sleeve back and glared at his watch. 'You can just make the four o'clock bus back to town if I drive you,' he said.

'No!' The word was torn from her, for she couldn't take any more of this cat-and-mouse game. Couldn't take any more of his unkindness. 'No, I won't leave until I know whether Sable was telling the truth.'

'What truth?' he rasped.

She whispered, 'That you lo—love me.' Flint remained as still as death.

'Why? So you can gloat over yet another conquest?' he jeered. 'Boast about it to your friends? First you have the famour Dexter Grant eating out of your hand, then his old friend falls madly in love with you. Not quite in the same league, but quite a record for your first summer among the glamour crowd.'

There was so much pain in his eyes that she involuntarily cried, 'Don't—don't, darling! It's not like that at all——'

'Isn't it?' He rounded on her, taking her by the shoulders, almost shaking her, and she started to cry because she had longed for him to touch her, but in this angry way. 'Isn't it? You said you wanted a taste of the glamorous life, and doesn't that include having guys fall all over themselves for you? Well, you managed it, Polly! Sure, I fell in love with you. I won't deny it, so you can chalk up another victory. The only difference between me and the rest of your admirers is that that I wish to God I *didn't* love you, and I intend to get over you as fast and as painlessly as I can. So you can count me out of your life. As far as you're concerned, I never existed.' He let go of her then, and turned away. It was the first time she had ever seen his broad shoulders droop.

'As far as *I'm* concerned, no one *else* exists. Flint, please look at me.' He turned to her again, but his face was austere, his brows furrowed. 'I've been an awful fool, Flint,' she said softly, 'but I love *you*. No one else. Just you.'

In the silence that followed she was aware of the repetitive chirping of a chickadee in the garden, then, 'How can I believe you, Polly?' he said quietly. 'Just because you've had a fight with Dexter——'

'But I haven't!' she cried. 'At least, that has nothing to do with it . . .'

'I'm not part of the world you long for,' he said. He was no longer angry, but deeply serious, and this frightened her more than his fury.

'I don't want that world, either.' Her eyes were bleak with distress. 'I thought I did, but I was wrong. Please, *please*, Flint! You *must* believe me,' and when he did not reply, she said, 'at least let me come here and see you. I couldn't bear never to see you. Now I know how you feel about me.'

'But I don't *want* you here, Polly,' he said, and she

recoiled as if he had slapped her. The chickadee flew away into the bushes.

'My bag's upstairs. I'll get it and go,' she said in a small, cold, even voice. She wouldn't beg him any more. She had more pride than that. Besides, she knew him. Knew his stubbornness. To beg would be as ineffectual as pounding her fists against an iron door. And she was damned if she was going to humble herself any more. She wasn't Marjorie Slater's daughter for nothing!

With leaden feet she fetched her bag from the airy blue and white bedroom and returned to the kitchen. He was standing with his back to the room, moodily staring out. He turned when he heard her stop.

'Do you *really* care for me, Polly?' he asked, and her heart stirred with hope at the naked need reflected on his face, but she hardened herself. He had put her through too much. She wasn't about to throw herself into his arms, no matter how ardently she might long to, so, 'There's no point in discussing it, Flint,' was all she could say. And then, before he could reply, she noticed a faint ribbon of smoke coming out of the oven and was aware of the smell of burning.

'My cake!' she wailed, dropping her bag and rushing towards the stove.

'Polly! No!' cried Flint, but he was too late and her wail turned into a scream as her bare hand touched the hot metal cake tin. She dropped the pan, and burnt sponge cake scattered over the kitchen floor.

'Polly!' His arm was round her waist, supporting her, for the pain was excruciating, and she stumbled as the room started to swim in an alarming manner. He half carried, half dragged her to the kitchen sink and turned on the cold water tap. 'Hold your hand under this,' he ordered, taking her wrist and holding it under the tap. 'That should help the pain and stop the blistering. The important thing is not to let the air get to it.'

The icy water felt horrible at first, and she whimpered through clenched teeth, but in a moment it acted like an anodyne on her burnt flesh, and the pain started to diminish. But she still felt sick and dizzy and, in spite of herself, a sob broke from her, and tears started to roll down her face.

Flint didn't say anything, but gently started to wipe her tears away with his fingers. She jerked her head back and he stopped.

When the cold water had done its work, he wrapped her poor hand in a clean dish towel. 'How do you feel now, Pollyanna?' he asked softly, and she thought that his use of that tender nickname was harder for her to bear than his coldness.

'I'll live!' she replied, and took an experimental step towards her bag. The floor seemed to rise up to meet her, and she nearly fell. He was at her side in an instant, sweeping her up into his strong arms, and she had to fight the desire to cling to him.

'You're still faint, Pollyanna. A little rest is indicated,' he said. He carried her into the den and laid her gently down on one of the large chintz sofas, plumping up a cushion and placing it behind her head. A kiss away. If she was going to faint, thought Polly, it was more likely to be from this proximity than from the shock of her accident. Her breath caught in her throat as he gently stroked the traces of tears on her pale cheeks.

'I can't bear to see you cry,' he said, his voice gruff and uneven. 'I can't bear it.'

Unresponsive to his gentle touch, she willed herself to lie motionless. 'You mustn't let it get to you. You intend to get over me fast and painlessly. Remember?'

He uttered a hoarse sound, a sound like a strangled sob. 'I'm such a fool, Pollyanna,' he said in that strange, ragged voice. 'I could no more get over you than I could get over *breathing*. You don't get over loving the right person quite as easily as that!'

'I know,' she said, pulling herself into a sitting position.

He sat back on his heels and regarded her through eyes

that were dark with emotion. 'I've been in hell these past weeks, Polly.'

Her child's mouth lifted in a ghost of a smile. 'I haven't exactly been in Paradise myself,' she said.

'I told myself I didn't care. That you were a silly girl taken in by glitter.' He leaned over and stroked a lock of hair that had fallen over her forehead, and this time she didn't draw away. 'But you're not taken in by it, are you?'

'Not any more. Not for a long time, actually.'

'Did you really only take the job with me because you wanted to get to know Dexter?' he asked.

For a second she was tempted to deny it, to save them both pain. But her natural honesty overcame her. 'At first,' she admitted, 'but only at first. I was dazzled— never anything more. I've been so . . .' she groped for a word, '. . . so *blind*. I didn't know what love was. I couldn't understand why kissing Dexter wasn't the same as kissing you.'

'I don't want to hear about you kissing Dexter,' Flint said fiercely. 'You belong to *me*. No one else.'

'I know that. I think I knew it that night on the island. . . only I didn't understand it then.' Her beautiful hazel eyes searched his face. 'Does that make sense?'

He nodded, 'I think so. It was the same for me that night. I didn't know what had hit me. I found out pretty quickly though, when you started carrying on with Dexter.'

'I *didn't* carry on——' she protested, but he continued, 'Carrying on or not, I've never felt so jealous in my life. I knew then that I was in love with you. And that what I felt was something I've never had for anyone else.'

'I had no idea you felt that way, darling,' she told him. 'After all, I thought you and Sable . . . well, she *was* living at Crabtree Farm, and . . .'

He raked his hand through his unruly red hair which, she now noticed, needed cutting, and lay on the back of his neck like a little boy's.

'I was afraid you'd think that,' he said, 'but I couldn't

say anything. I'd promised Sable.'

'Promised her what?' Her eyes might still be dim with tears but her heart was flying again.

'Sable's loved Dexter for years,' he said, 'but he never seemed to notice her—not as a woman, that is.' He pulled himself up to sit facing her on the sofa. 'And then, you may or may not recall, he got himself entangled with a redhead for a brief spell.'

'The day I came for my bike!' Polly exclaimed, 'I remember.'

'Yeah! Well, Sable was very upset, so she came out to lick her wounds at the farm. She figured that if she disappeared off the scene for a bit, Dexter might start missing her. Start showing some interest. So she made me promise not to tell a soul how she felt about Dexter. Because she knows him. If the girl plays hard to get, he's keen.'

'Yes,' agreed Polly, recalling her scuffles with the actor.

'Then,' Flint went on, 'he fell for you! We hadn't planned on *that*!'

'Poor Sable.' Polly's pale cheeks blushed pink.

'Poor *me*!' Flint growled. 'I was head over heels in love with you by this time. I could have have murdered both of you!'

'Hang on a moment!' She drew up her knees and leaned forward. 'I heard you *begging* Sable to stay on here. How do you explain that?'

He grinned ruefully. 'I needed her here to protect me,' he said.

'*Protect* you!' Her mouth opened in astonishment. 'Protect you from what?'

'From you.' She stared at him blankly and he gave a low chuckle. 'You still don't seem to realise how attractive you are, Pollyanna,' he said. 'If I'd been alone with you here, I would have wound up making love to you. You're so sexy, honey. Such a *woman*. I knew I wouldn't have been able to leave you alone, and I was

afraid I'd scare you away. Besides, it didn't seem fair.
You trusted me and I didn't want to spoil that. So I asked
Sable to stick around to protect us. She thought it was a
hoot! They don't act like that in the sophisticated world
she inhabits.'

'So that's why she called you "old fashioned",' Polly
said, a great weight lifting off her heart. 'I thought it was
because you didn't want her to pursue a career.'

'I don't care whether she has a career or not, I'm not
marrying Sable. I'm marrying you.' Flint laced his
fingers through her uninjured hand. 'I am, aren't I,
Pollyanna?' he said softly.

She looked up into his irregular, craggy face through a
blur of sudden tears. 'Oh, please—yes . . .' she stammered, unable to say more. Then, 'Oh! But my cooking
course! I'm supposed to start cookery school in
September.'

'Well, is there a rule that says married ladies can't
attend?' he asked. 'It simply means we'll get married this
month.' He became serious. 'I don't want to rush you,
sweetheart,' he said, 'but I—I *need* you. I'm only half a
person when you're not there.'

'It's the same for me,' Polly smiled. 'I don't mind being
rushed.'

He started caressing the inside of her arm and she
tingled with pleasure. 'I'm glad you're taking that course,
Polly,' he said. 'I hoped you would when I sent that
cheque. But please,' he looked at her intently, as if he
wanted to memorise her face, 'please try not to rush off
the minute you graduate.'

'Darling! Why should I?' she asked, startled.

'Oh, to become a master chef at the Ritz, or take a job
in Paris,' he teased. But his eyes were serious.

'I'll settle for becoming master chef at Crabtree Farm,'
she assured him. 'It's all I've ever wanted—and children.
We will have children, won't we, Flint?'

He smiled and kissed the tip of her nose. 'A couple,
Pollyanna. When we've had a bit of time to ourselves.

But we'd better get married first! Perhaps we could be married in England, since I don't imagine your mother's too keen on formal weddings.'

'You can meet all my relatives,' Polly cried delightedly, 'they'll love you.'

'That's nice. But the important thing is—do *you* love me, Pollyanna? Nothing else matters in the world.'

She stroked his cheek and a tremor passed through him. 'I told you before,' she whispered, 'I love you with all my heart.'

'And you forgive me for being so cruel . . . when I first found you here?'

'I forgive you, darling.'

'I was mad with jealousy. I—I wasn't thinking straight,' he muttered huskily, and she said,

'Just promise that you won't send me away—ever again.'

Putting his arms around her, Flint gently pushed her back on to the cushions, his mouth claimed hers, and she forgot the ache in her hand, the room, everything except his lips, and the thudding of his heart against her own.

'You do realise that we're alone here?' he said, when the kiss came to an end. 'No Sable to protect you.'

'Come here, you fool!' she whispered, and he stretched out beside her. 'Do you remember, when you first met me you told Dexter you thought I was the type who was hard to get rid of?' He started to say 'Oh, sweetheart . . .' but she put her fingers on his lips. 'Shh! You were *right*, I am! You'll never get rid of me now.'

'I think,' said Flint, kissing her between words, 'I think that's an excellent arrangement.'

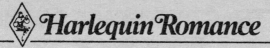 **Harlequin Romance**

Coming Next Month

Available in May wherever paperback books are sold, or
through Harlequin Reader Service.

In the U.S.
901 Fuhrmann Blvd.
P.O. Box 1397
Buffalo, N.Y. 14240-1397

In Canada
P.O. Box 603
Fort Erie, Ontario
L2A 5X3

ATTRACTIVE, SPACE SAVING BOOK RACK

Display your most prized novels on this handsome and sturdy book rack. The hand-rubbed walnut finish will blend into your library decor with quiet elegance, providing a practical organizer for your favorite hard-or soft-covered books.

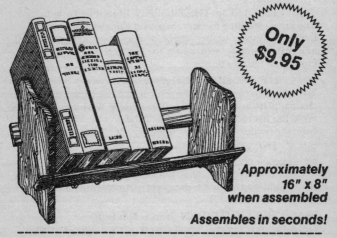

Only $9.95

Approximately 16" x 8" when assembled

Assembles in seconds!

To order, rush your name, address and zip code, along with a check or money order for $10.70* ($9.95 plus 75¢ postage and handling) payable to *Harlequin Reader Service*:

Harlequin Reader Service
Book Rack Offer
901 Fuhrmann Blvd.
P.O. Box 1325
Buffalo, NY 14269-1325

Offer not available in Canada.

BKR-1R

*New York residents add appropriate sales tax.